**

Leave it to me to finally learn how to drive stick...with a woman who's nothing but trouble.

Protecting people is what I do. But with Gemma everything is different. There was a time when she was my everything and I would have given my life to protect her.

Now she's back and this time I won't fail her. I'm ready to put it all on the line to keep her safe.

My past finally caught up with me and I had to make a choice. Leave or destroy my family. I'll do anything to keep them safe...including walk into enemy territory.

Sinful is the conclusion to the Sin Duet.

SINFUL

M. MALONE
NANA MALONE

ALSO BY M. MALONE & NANA MALONE

- The Shameless Trilogy -

Shame (prequel)

Shameless / Shameful / UnAshamed

- The Force Duet -

Forcful (prequel)

Force / Enforce

- The Deep Duet -

In Deep (prequel)

Deep / Deeper

- The Sin Duet -

Beyond Sin (prequel)

Sin / Sinful

1

Gemma

Chaos.

Blood.

So. Much. Blood.

Noah lay on the ground writhing and clutching his shoulder while a small pool of dark red liquid proceeded to stain the polished hardwood.

I was a trained operative; the sight of blood shouldn't turn my stomach, but it had my gut twisting into a knot.

Maybe because you know this is your fault.

What the fuck had I said wrong? What had set him off? This wasn't my Matthias. This was someone else.

Someone far more dangerous. And I wasn't sure I could reach that person.

My eyes darted up to Matthias, and I held my hands up. "Matthias, listen to me." I hoped that by using his name I could get through to him. The look in his eyes was all wildness and tortured pain. I had to try and bring him back.

Rafe, however, wasn't bothering with the talky-talky route. Instead, he slowly approached Matthias, looking calm and cool, his hands up as if in surrender, but his gaze never wavered. I could tell by the way he moved, weight on the balls of his feet, slowly, deliberately, that he was poised to spring at any moment.

Matthias's gaze darted from me to Rafe and back again as if judging who the larger threat was. As if he were weighing who might do more harm to him. I certainly didn't want him thinking it was me.

When Rafe spoke, his voice was low. "Matthias. Kid, it's okay. No one's going to hurt you. Just put the knife down, okay? We can talk about this. I know you didn't mean to hurt Noah."

From the ground, Noah moaned. "It's okay. Just listen to Rafe. You can... trust him." Noah's head fell back as if the effort to speak had taken all of his strength.

I inched forward as Rafe moved. If I could get to

Matthias first, then maybe Rafe wouldn't kill him. *Would* Rafe kill him? He was part of the team, but from some things Matthias had said, I understood there was some animosity between them.

But was it worth killing over? Noah said to trust Rafe, but hell, I didn't trust anybody. Especially not with Matthias. He meant too much to me.

I took another step forward. "Matthias. It'll be okay if you just put the knife down. I know you don't want to hurt anybody. This was an accident. It was my fault. I should have told you everything once I knew who you were. If you can just breathe and relax, we can talk about it, okay?"

Rafe's voice was low. "That's right. Listen to Gemma. Listen to Noah, kid. Nice and easy. Put the knife down. It's not worth it."

I studied Matthias closely, praying, hoping that I was getting through to him. Though Noah was clearly awake and alert, watching everything from the ground, he was still bleeding heavily. His gaze flickered to me, then Matthias, then Rafe, and back to me. Maybe he was trying to figure out what his chances were and who he needed to rely on.

"Listen, Matthias. I'm the one you're mad at. I know I broke your trust. Just relax. If you want to stay mad, stay mad at me. I messed this up." I inched toward him as he approached the door. "Just put the knife down and we can talk. Okay?"

For a moment, I thought he was going to listen. I thought I was getting through to him. For a moment, I could see the man I loved. But then he shifted his eyes again, and he was gone. Those eyes that I loved, so bright and insightful, turned cold and dark again.

Matthias was gone. The cold-blooded killer they called The Shadow was there in his place. Then in the blink of an eye, he was out the door. I heard, rather than saw, the scuffle in the hallway. Then I heard more groaning. When I ran out the door, I saw Oskar holding his nose and trying to get up off the ground. Diana kneeled next to him holding a cloth to his face.

Jesus Christ, what had I done?

I could have gone after him. But there were people here who needed me. *Bleeding* people.

I turned and ran back into the room where Noah was. Rafe was by his side pressing something over the wound, and his free hand held his phone at his ear. "Dr. Breckner, we need you here at the penthouse. There's been an incident."

My gaze darted back to the door. Did I still have time? Could I still go after him?

On the ground, Noah groaned and glared at me.

Through clenched teeth he spoke. "You stay here. Do *not* go after him. You still have questions to answer."

My gaze darted back to the exit. I didn't take my orders from him. But this was Matthias's family. If anyone could help me get him back, it would be them.

Besides, as fast as he was, Matthias was probably in the wind by now anyway. I ran into the hallway and then into the kitchen to grab an icepack and some towels before running to the big, brawny German. "I'm guessing you'll need this?"

Oskar pushed himself up into a sitting position and winked at me. "Are you worried about me, beautiful? Not to worry. Your boyfriend barely touched me."

"I don't know. That's a lot of blood, Oskar."

"Don't worry. I'll stay just as pretty. If you're looking to upgrade your boyfriend experience, I at least promise I won't try to kill you after."

I knew he was kidding, but at the same time, it made me feel worse. This was all my fault. What had I done? I'd been juggling too many balls, and now people were going to die, all because I'd followed orders. *Maybe it's time to stop following orders.*

Maybe it was time to go on instinct, because my instincts were probably the only things that were going to save me. I was in a den full of killers. Only my wits were going to get me out alive, because even though Matthias had just lost his mind, these people cared about him. Deeply. And I'd been the cause of all this.

I knew they were going to make me pay, one way or another. And I'd take whatever punishment they wanted to dole out. But first we needed to get Matthias back. Then they could do whatever they wanted to do with me. All I cared about in that moment was him.

———

Matthias

BLOOD.

Confusion.

Pain.

What the fuck had I just done? Noah. I'd fucking stabbed Noah.

Was he dead? Had I killed him? It was like a part of my brain had known what was happening. I could see it all in sickening slow motion. The slice of the blade. The warmth of my mentor's blood. But I'd still been powerless to stop what I was doing.

Noah. Rafe. Gemma. People I cared about and

trusted. Well, okay. Not Gemma... or Rafe. But Noah. I would *never* hurt Noah.

But you did. And now you have to leave.

Everything I'd done, everything I'd tried to atone for... All gone up in a puff of smoke. Would there ever be forgiveness for someone like me?

No. *Assassins don't get forgiveness. Just because you pretend to be the good guy now doesn't mean you are.*

I went on semi-autopilot as my subconscious took me on a route I'd taken hundreds of times mentally. To the casual observer (and I hoped a trained assassin), it might look like I was wandering the streets. But I had a destination in mind. I knew where I was going. I hadn't been there in over a year, but I knew the way. I knew why I needed to be there. *Safety.* I paid a pretty penny to keep the flat in the city.

The landlord asked me constantly if I wanted to sublet the place, but I'd always said no. I couldn't take the risk of someone possibly finding my cache of weapons, my cash, my passports... Those things in the wrong hands would be catastrophic, and not just for me.

No, it was better that I kept it empty. Because right then, that flat was exactly what I needed. A place to lay low, a place to think, someplace away from everything and everyone. But no matter the distance I put between me and the penthouse, I couldn't escape my thoughts.

How could you do it? Noah protected you. He loved you like a brother.

I ran a hand through my hair, trying to block out the voices, the ones that told me I fucked up, the ones that that told me that I'd just destroyed the only family I'd ever had.

This is safety. Survive. Worry about the rest later. It was what Noah would tell me. So that's what I did.

I kept my hands tucked in my pockets on the subway so no one would see the blood. Once I got to my stop, I hopped out, kept my head down, and pulled my cap over my head.

For years, I'd hunted the bad guys. I'd stopped them from hurting people. I'd made sure the innocents stayed safe. Now, *I* was the bad guy.

I let myself in the flat and engaged the dead bolt. I'd taken all sorts of evasive measures, but I hadn't felt anyone following me.

In a perfunctory manner, I hit the shower, washing all traces of blood off of my body. I took my clothes, shoved them in a bag and carried them to the dumpster three blocks from the flat. I didn't want anything leading anyone back to the place in case I needed it again.

You won't need it again. You aren't coming back here. This is it. Say goodnight. I'd spent enough time pretending I was one of the normals. Clearly, I wasn't.

Once I came back from my clothing disposal, I grabbed one of the duffels from the closet and then went out into the living room. My phone rang on the small coffee table at the center of the room, and I froze. How had I left it on? Did they know where I was? When I grabbed it to remove the SIM card, I saw Gemma's face, and my heart squeezed.

She'd lied to me. She'd been acting this whole time. The lies and betrayal, they stung the worst. It hurt the worst. I would never be able to look at her the same way after I discovered she'd been working for Ian.

Not to worry, mate. You're never going to see her again. I ended the call and took out the SIM and battery on the phone.

My next step was in the kitchen. I moved the trash can from its spot next to the refrigerator and made a fist, marking along the wall. Then I pulled back my hand and punched precisely where my fist had been. The drywall splattered, bits of it flying around everywhere. When I reached inside, I pulled out what I needed, my ghost stash. I had a few ghost stashes all over the city, just in case.

This one had a hundred thousand dollars and a few passports, just what I needed to get the hell out of Dodge. Life as an assassin had paid very, very well.

Unfortunately, life as an assassin had also made it impossible to sleep.

I shoved the money into the duffel bag along with some warmer clothes. For a second, I considered going back. They might forgive me.

There were eight passports with various names. Different variations of me could be seen in each of them: the dyed hair, the contacts—all of them me, all of them a killer. Could I go back? Was it possible I hadn't hurt Noah after all? The monster had taken over for just a few minutes, and I couldn't be certain exactly what had gone down.

The pain inside of my head pierced sharply. *Fuck*. I dropped to my knees as I held my head and groaned, moaning, begging for it to stop, praying for it to end. What the hell?

There is no going home.

No one loves you.

You're not worth anything.

No. Noah had told me—more pain. Sharper than the last time. *Motherfucker*. I stopped thinking about Noah and Gemma and started thinking about the safe house where I'd be able to sleep and rest. Finally, the pain dissipated until it was barely a dull throb. Jesus fucking Christ.

Okay then, no thinking of that other place. Just move forward. No looking back.

Absolutely not. I had to get the hell out of there, because whether I liked it or not, Blake Security was as good as I was. If they were looking for me, they'd find me if I stayed put. I had to get on the move, or survival wasn't going to be an option.

2

Gemma

I CROSSED my arms and hugged myself tight as the adrenaline high of the previous ten minutes finally crashed. It was like coming down from a chemical high. My blood ran hot, then ice-cold. Colors and sounds flashed through my mind as I started shaking violently.

What the hell had just happened?

Hearing a slight noise to my left, I opened my eyes and saw Oskar trying to pull himself to a standing position. He was a big guy, and it obviously took a lot of muscle to move all that bulk around. Despite his earlier bravado, he was in pain if the look on his face was any indication. Then I noticed why. There was glass on the floor surrounding him and he was pulling himself right through it.

Delaney appeared at his elbow and talked to him in a low voice. After a moment, he took the blond giant's arm and helped Oskar stand. Then he glanced around the room, and his dark eyes reflected the same horror I felt.

It really was a mess.

Chairs were overturned, and there was glass everywhere, the shimmer of light on the shards blinding. My mouth fell open. A tornado would have caused less damage. How was it I hadn't noticed the level of destruction before?

You were too focused on Matthias.

As it was, nothing in the room seemed to have escaped the path of destruction.

"Oh Matthias... What happened?" I whispered.

As I shifted, my foot kicked something hard. Shards of wood littered the floor. Was that from the coffee table? I examined the piece of wood dispassionately. It was hard to get my thoughts to flow properly when all I could think of was the look in Matthias's eyes. They'd been dead. Cold. That man had been more than capable of murder.

I shivered. It hadn't been the man I loved behind those eyes anymore.

Love?

Just the thought caught me off guard. Had I fallen that far down the rabbit hole? I couldn't pinpoint the moment when I'd lost myself, but I knew that it shredded me to not see any hint of him in his expression before he'd run.

Truthfully, there had been nothing there at all. No emotion. No conscience. It was as if the man I knew had been deleted, leaving nothing but a cold, empty killing machine.

You drove him to this. Your lies sent him over the edge.

I put a shaky hand to my forehead as I tried to stand, ignoring the twinge in my ankle. I'd probably twisted it slightly in the chaos, but compared to everyone else in the room, my problems were minor.

Noah was still on the ground while Rafe applied pressure to his wound and, barked orders to everyone around him. Afraid to get too close and possibly distract him, I peered around Rafe's broad shoulders trying to see Noah's face. Was he breathing?

God help them all if he wasn't. No matter what I'd just seen, I knew Matthias would never want to hurt his friend. If he came back and found out Noah was dead, I wasn't sure what he'd do. Probably go on a bender that made this one look like a toddler throwing a tantrum.

There was a ding, and I walked toward the elevator but stopped short when a pair of broad shoulders filled my vision.

Delaney glared down at me. "It's the doctor. I'll let him in."

Well, all right then. That answered my question of whether anyone had filled him in. It was stupid to hope that maybe I'd have the chance to explain before they all passed judgment, but this was the way of life as an ORUS agent. My role was to complete my mission, not to make friends while doing it.

But admit it, you were enjoying having friends for a while. I shook off the thought. My time was coming to have the normal life I'd always dreamed of. But I had responsibilities to complete first. I just hoped that they hadn't driven Matthias away from me completely.

The doctor came in, and Delaney led him to the office. He immediately took the stethoscope from around his neck when he saw Noah on the floor. To my surprise and extreme relief, Noah was awake. But instead of calming him, the sight of the doctor seemed to agitate Noah more, and he struggled against Rafe's hold and started yelling.

"Don't let her leave," was the last thing I heard before Oskar turned in my direction.

I shrank back and then parked it on the couch Oskar pointed to.

"Yeah, you aren't going anywhere," he snarled. His earlier kindness was gone now that he knew I was the one who'd triggered this destruction. "Not sure what the fuck you just did to Matthias, but you're not leaving until we get some answers."

Answers. If they were looking to me for answers, they were going to be sorely disappointed. Not only had I been just as shocked by Matthias's behavior as everyone else, but considering he'd looked ready to kill me too, I was just as confused as they were.

But I was an ORUS agent, and I didn't have time to ruminate on my feelings. There was a mission to complete, after all. And although the new Orion wasn't as much of a jackass as the previous leader, Ian was still the head of the organization. He would want an update so he could determine the next steps they would take.

"You'll get your answers as soon as I have some. But that means I have to check in." I pulled out my phone. But before I could dial, Oskar leaned over and snatched it.

"Hey! What are you doing?"

"Keeping you from calling any more of your cronies in to finish the job."

I glared at him and then glanced over to the office where Noah was now sitting up with his shirt off. With his naked torso on display, I could tell that he was a former agent. He had a bullet wound scar on one of his shoulders and now a sizeable gash above his heart, near his collarbone. It must not have been that bad though, since the doctor was currently dressing it and not taking him to the medical bay.

"Bring her here," Noah said. His voice was weak, but we could all hear him clearly.

Oskar wasted no time and dragged me to my feet. Even though he was taking me against my will, his touch was still gentle.

Noah glared up at me.

"Was that your mission, Gemma? Did Ian send you here to take us out? Or to turn Matthias against us? Not sure what the hell you could have said to him to make him go off like that. I've never seen him that far gone." Noah shook his head.

I wasn't sure what that meant, but it probably wasn't anything good. Not for me at least. Because if they had no clue what was wrong with Matthias, that meant they had little hope of helping him.

"My mission had nothing to do with turning

Matthias against anyone. And in case you hadn't noticed, I was in just as much danger as the rest of you."

Noah's forehead crinkled in thought. "Yeah. I noticed that." He exchanged a dark look with Rafe who shook his head slowly.

"Look. All I want to do is contact Ian and let him know what's going on. You know how this works. I only have the information I'm given to complete the mission. If you want the real story, that's above my pay grade."

After a long, tense moment, Noah looked over at Oskar and raised an eyebrow. The blond grunted and handed back my phone. Reluctantly.

"But you call him here and now. You're not going off somewhere by yourself until we know what the hell is going on." Noah stared at me pointedly, and I nodded.

Oskar smiled again. "Until further notice, you're under house arrest with Blake Security. But tell Ian not to worry. We'll keep his little spy safe and sound."

My heart sank.

It looked like Ian's reaction to my mission failure was the least of my problems.

———

Gemma

I ACCEPTED my phone back from Oskar with hesitation. This was not a conversation I was looking forward to. However, Ian was not a patient man, so I might as well get it over with.

Ian's number was the last I'd called from this particular burner phone. I hit the number and let it ring a certain number of times and then immediately called back.

Ian answered with his usual grunt. "What's your status?"

"We have a situation," I responded slowly, turning my back so I could talk without Oskar glaring directly in my face. Not that it helped much. Now I was facing Noah and Rafe. The doctor looked between them all warily as he continued to bind Noah's ribs. My mind locked-on to the rhythmic motion as the white bandage wound around and around.

I let the soothing sight of that fabric traveling around Noah calm my mind before responding. "Matthias is in the wind."

I pulled the phone away from myself at the loud expletive that came over the line. As Ian ranted, I sighed. Noah and Rafe continued to glare. When the noise finally subsided, I put the phone back to my ear.

"What the fuck happened? You had the target on lock."

"I don't know exactly what happened yet, but my identity was compromised. He was upset. Then it was like a switch flipped, and he was enraged. One minute he was normal, and then the next he was trying to kill everyone."

"Put Noah on the phone," Ian gritted out.

I winced and then held the phone out slowly in Noah's direction. "Orion wants to speak with you."

But it was Rafe who spoke up, loud enough for Ian to hear. Purposefully, I was quite sure.

"Orion can fuck off. We don't answer to him. We're not his toy soldiers anymore."

I winced at the description, but having heard some of Rafe's and Noah's stories, I could understand their frustration. Hadn't I also become disillusioned with the way ORUS played with our lives, treating us like disposable resources? Wasn't that why I'd been working so hard and strategizing ways I could disappear and live a different life?

Every time I thought of it, I felt so disloyal. Andromeda had sacrificed so much to keep me, even moving her partner and me to a remote island in Canada for a while so I could grow up without anyone in ORUS finding out. Once I'd been old enough,

Andromeda had trained me, harder and faster than any other recruit, so I would never again be vulnerable. Never again be a victim. And how was I going to repay the woman who had saved me?

By defecting as soon as I can.

I pulled the phone back, but then Noah shook his head. He tried to reach for the phone and then groaned as the motion pulled at his shoulder. Finally, Rafe stepped forward, took the phone, and put it on speaker. He didn't look happy about it, though.

"What do you want, Ian?" Noah said.

"Just to talk. This situation isn't ideal for either of us. We've worked together before. I think we can help each other in this instance."

"Not sure what you're proposing we do. If Matthias doesn't want to be found, then he won't be. And if you think I'm going to help you track the kid down, then all that power really has gone to your head."

Ian's breathing was the only thing they could hear over the line for a minute. "This is a courtesy I'm extending you, Blake. But you and I both know I'm not asking."

Well, hell. I instinctively took a step back. Throwing an alpha male statement like that into this kind of room was like detonating a bomb. Noah sat up taller, like he could physically intimidate even over the phone. Rafe bared his teeth and Oskar crossed his beefy arms. Delaney still stood near the entrance to the room, but he wore the same stoic expression as before. Like he was prepared to fight to the death anyway.

It was like watching a pack of predators all circling the same piece of meat. Guaranteed not to end well for anyone. At least not without massive amounts of bloodshed.

Finally, Noah said, "If you go after my man, it will end in blood. And I'm not talking about his. You sent an ORUS agent into my house."

All eyes swung to me. It took all my training to hold my expression. I would not show fear. If they got even a whiff of it, they'd pounce on the weakness. Until they knew what the hell had happened with Matthias, I had to keep it together.

"My only interest is to get Matthias off the street before bodies start to drop. Once we have him contained, then you and I can talk." Ian's voice jumped, making him sound like he was running.

He must be on the move. I could only hope he wasn't coming here.

"I'll let you know what we find." Noah nodded at the phone again, and Rafe hit the button to hang up.

I bet Ian loved that. He was probably chewing nails. A rogue, former ORUS agent was off the map and possibly about to unleash destruction on the streets of New York City. No wonder Ian had sounded like he was running. If anyone would be a target for a rogue Matthias, the head of the organization that had ruined his life would be at the top of the list.

Noah seemed to have the same thought because he looked at Rafe and said, "Get eyes on Ian. Maybe we'll get lucky and Matthias will show up. This might be our last chance to catch him before he truly goes off grid."

"Got it." Rafe handed him the phone and then walked out of the room. Oskar stepped forward.

It was amusing how they accused ORUS of treating them like toy soldiers, but they all reported to Noah the same way. They were still soldiers doing the bidding of the monarchy.

But now, Noah Blake was their king.

"Take her to the medical wing. And secure it this time. Until we know what's happening, we don't want her causing any more trouble."

I rolled my eyes. "So I'm a prisoner for real?"

Oskar winked. "You're lucky. If Matthias's knife had been a few inches lower, you wouldn't be going to the medical wing right now."

He gestured for me to precede him. It was tempting to resist just to see what he'd do but I was suddenly exhausted. Plus, I didn't want them to be my enemies.

All I wanted was to find out what happened with Matthias, figure out how to undo my devil's bargain with the Family, and somehow escape it all unscathed.

But I couldn't accomplish any of that right now and definitely not when I was so tired I felt like collapsing. So I walked down the corridor that led to the medical wing I'd stayed in when I'd first come here. The whole time, I was acutely aware of Oskar following close on my heels.

When we reached the room, I whirled around at the sound of the door slamming behind me. Oskar's face appeared in the glass panel on the door. It shouldn't have been so creepy the way he was staring, but it made me feel like a science experiment.

"You said if Matthias's knife had been lower, I wouldn't be going to the medical wing right now," I challenged. "Where would I be going then?"

Oskar smiled slowly. "Into a body bag."

Then he was gone, leaving me locked in the cold, sterile room.

$$3$$

Matthias

I woke on the floor next to the bed curled up into a ball. Rays of sunlight streaked into the flat, and I had to squint against the blinding light of it.

What the fuck had happened?

As I pushed myself into a sitting position, I did my mental pat down for the weapons strapped to my body and then reached up to the bedside table for my gun. I breathed a sigh of relief. Everything was where it should be. As it always did, slowly, bits and pieces of the day before started coming back to me.

I remembered waking up, wrapped around

Gemma, and seeing the tattoos on the back of her neck. Even now, it made my stomach roil and knot and bunch and squeeze, making me want to shoot out bile through my esophagus. How had I been so wrong about her?

Well, it's easy. Your instincts told you not to trust her. But you listened to your dick.

Yeah, note to self: stop listening to dick.

The problem was that with Gemma it felt like it was more than my dick, like what was happening with us was way more than just physical. My brain wanted to spend the time dissecting the threads, unraveling each one as it led to what she said that might be the truth and what she said that was a lie. Fact or fiction. Could I even decipher it?

No time for that. Assess the situation. Move on.

"Fuck. Get your shit together, mate."

I pushed myself into a sitting position. Then I steadied my breathing. In for three, hold for three, out for three. I'd learned to meditate during my training. Sometimes it helped me see more clearly.

After I'd found out who she was, we'd gone to the office. I'd dragged her in to talk to Noah and Rafe, the rage I was carrying around lingering just under the surface.

Despite the colossal fuckup of fucking the enemy,

neither of them called me out for being an epic knob-head and putting the whole company at risk.

Both of them were on my side, trying to figure out who would send Gemma to infiltrate us and why she was there—what the Family wanted with me, what ORUS might want with me, etc. And then...

A sharp pain pierced the fleshy brain matter behind my eyeball as I tried to fit the pieces together again. But unlike yesterday, I didn't black out; I fought the pain.

Breathe in, breathe out. Breathe in, breathe out. Focus. Breath by breath, moment by moment, the pain receded, and I started to see with clarity. Something had happened in that office. Something I couldn't remember.

And afterward... *chaos.*

The rage I kept locked away—my monster. Someone had unlocked the door and coaxed it out with the promise of fresh meat, and I'd been helpless to do anything about it. Mentally, I'd tried to lock the monster back in. But once the dragon was out, there was really no containing it. And only death and destruction followed behind it.

There had been a fight... and then...

Dread unfurled in my gut as the memory became clear.

I'd stabbed Noah. My mentor. The man who'd saved

my life. The man who was so much more than a mate to me. He was my brother. *Shit.*

Noah.

I itched to pick up the phone and call, to check in, to assess if Noah was okay. Under normal circumstances, even in a fight, I was cold, clinical. Because my directive was no longer to kill, I usually opted to maim. Unless someone was trying to kill me, in which case, killing was on the table.

But Noah wouldn't have been trying to kill me. *I would have known that, right?* So maybe I'd only given him a wound that was enough to hurt him, but not kill him.

I hoped.

Come on, think, think, think. Everyone in that building knew basic CPR. The ones with field experience—Rafe, Jonas, and Dylan—they would know what to do. How to patch the wound, etc. Then they would have called Breckner. They would have saved him. Besides, when I got settled, I could just hack in and check for myself.

Do not hack in.

There was always the chance that one of those knuckleheads had been paying attention on how to track people. Without me, it would take a while. But it could still be done, and I didn't have the requisite equipment to hack in super-stealth mode before I left.

You just have to walk away from this one.

I hated that idea, but I knew it was what I needed to do. I pushed myself to standing and forced myself to get ready. I didn't have long. If I'd left any traces of myself, it wouldn't be long before Rafe came knocking, or worse... *Ian.*

All along, Gemma had been working for that man. And to be honest, I had no beef with Ian. We had no quarrel. But Ian stood for everything that I'd had to walk away from, the death, the destruction...

Focus. Get your shit together, mate.

While I didn't have the equipment to penetrate the penthouse because the firewalls I'd set up were too strong, I did have a laptop, which meant I could manage basic things.

I knew I was asking for trouble, but I needed to do this.

Once I showered, got dressed, shoved some field provisions into my mouth, and guzzled half a gallon of water, I cracked open the laptop.

The guys would be looking for me on commercial airlines. They would also be looking for me to cross a border in one of the traditional ways—or at least that would be the standard practice. Or they would be looking for flight plans, private airstrips, anything that would lead them to me. I understood the rules and how the game was played. I was dangerous, and they needed to *contain* me.

And because you're dangerous, you need to be kept away from the rest of mankind.

With a few quick taps of my keyboard and skirting a couple of firewalls, I had what I needed. Access to the ORUS-operated airstrip. It was one I'd used before when I'd been an ORUS agent. Agents in upstate New York used it all the time.

The key was to hop on the flight that was already going out. Because if I deleted the flight, or caused a big commotion taking a whole lot of people out, there would be a whole lot of pissed-off assassins looking for me. But I was smart, so I'd simply change the flight time and give myself more time to get there.

I quickly scanned the flight plans. There was a flight leaving tonight. It would take a while, but I had time to kill. The best way to go upstate was probably to hop the train somewhere in Long Island and then head for the airstrip. There was a flight scheduled to leave at eleven, which meant flight checks and stuff would happen around ten. Which meant I should show up at eight and merely *borrow* the plane from the US government. Easy peasy.

Most flights were fueled automatically after landing,

so I wouldn't have to worry about fuel, at least not where I was going.

Time was my friend. The more distance I could put between me and the people I loved, the better things would be for everyone.

The memories slid into my consciousness again; Noah's face as I stabbed him, the confusion, the pain, the concern. I knew Noah well enough to know that the concern hadn't been for his own well-being.

Noah had been worried about me. Even in that moment, when the person he'd mentored stabbed him, Noah had been worried about me, as if that wasn't the most fucked up thing of all.

The effort of trying to remember exactly what happened took its toll, and my head throbbed. Quickly, I checked the train schedules and noted that I had three hours to catch the next one, which meant I had time for a quick nap. Because even though I'd only been up for a short time, the exhaustion of the last day was already dragging me under.

For the time being, I'd have to take this short rest, but soon... soon, I could really rest. I'd be away from all this. This was what I should have done a long time ago, taken that monster and separated it from as much human contact as possible. It was the only safe thing to do. And it was best for everyone.

———

Matthias

THE KEY to making most plans work was to alter them as little as possible from the original. I understood that, which was why I was sticking with the ORUS-approved flight plan and just leaving a couple of hours earlier. I notified the airport that there was a change in schedule over ORUS-approved channels, and now all I had to do was steal the plane. I knew I hadn't been followed from the flat, but I still had to be careful.

As far as ORUS was concerned, everything was locked tight. And it should be. I'd built their system. I'd set up the firewalls. There was a chance that ORUS had changed the security protocols since I was last on site, but there was a chance they hadn't, and I was banking on that. Until it was go-time, ORUS generally liked to leave things unmanned.

As far as anyone else knew, it was just a warehouse, locked tight. There were electrically charged fences around it, and there were cameras everywhere. Lucky for me, I knew how to exploit those.

Standing in one of the blind spots of the cameras

behind the building, I opened my laptop and got to work. The first step was recording a loop of the surrounding area and letting it run for ten minutes. Then it was time to do the real work.

It never ceased to amaze me, the buzz I got from hacking into something. What was that? Oh, you know, just my sociopathic tendencies coming out to play. There was an electrical charge to knowing I was going somewhere I wasn't supposed to. And what do you know? ORUS hadn't changed anything. There were passwords, of course, but ones with encryption protocols. It would take me less than a minute to get in because I'd set them up. It was hard to believe that Ian hadn't gotten the shit sorted and reorganized. If I were in charge of their security, I would change out all these protocols.

Anyone could have access to their whole system. Not that anyone would even dare. And anyone who tried would end up dead.

But, you know, just saying, change the protocols already.

In less than five minutes, I was in. *Perfect.* Then I inserted the loop into the video and turned off those damn cameras. In another thirty seconds, I was ready to go. I walked straight to the gate, pressed in the code, and I was in.

Once in the hangar, I helped myself to a little thing called a plane.

No one would miss it. A JSTAR. Lucky for me, I'd flown one before. If ORUS had changed out the plane, or used something else, it would have been a little bit more complicated. But it was almost as if Ian knew I'd need this plane eventually.

Once I performed all the safety checks, I checked my time. I still had minutes to spare. With the hangar door open, I said a silent prayer to a God I believed in and then started to taxi.

As the plane's wheels lifted off the ground, I rubbed at the ache in my chest. Ever since I'd woken up that morning, I'd had that yearning, the worry, and the panic. Was Noah okay? Was Gemma? What had Rafe done to her?

It's not your concern. She lied, remember?

Yes, she lied. I had to remember that, but I did care about her. And there was a part of me that worried about her still, because maybe she hadn't meant to get into any of this. Maybe, like me, she'd gotten caught up as a byproduct of her association with the Family. *Whether she would have or could have, the reality is you're here now.* It was over, because at the end of the day, I'd hurt Noah. There was no going back from that.

What I was doing was best for everyone. Even if

Noah had survived and Rafe hadn't killed Gemma, even if time magically rewound to three days ago before I discovered all her secrets, I was still dangerous.

My monster was out now, and there was no shoving him back in the cage. The searing pain in my skull when I thought about going back to help them had dulled significantly. Maybe with time, it would go away. But still, I understood what it meant. Whatever protocols I'd put in charge of my psychopathic monster, those were done. There was no going home again when my switch had been flipped to *kill, kill, kill* all the time.

I had to protect everyone from that.

As much as Noah had tried to save me from myself, as much as Lucia and JJ and Diana had helped softened my edges, and as much as I'd learned to form friendships with people like Oskar, the truth of it was, I was a killer. Always a killer.

There was no changing me. I had to put as much distance between me and them as humanly possible. It was for their own good. If I had to protect them from me, then I would, because at the end of the day, they were my family. And after what I'd done, I didn't trust myself with them. Never mind how they felt about it. This was in the best interest of everyone.

Are you sure about that?

4

———

Gemma

THE MEDICAL BAY was just as boring and uncomfortable as the last time I was there. There was nothing but a bed and various types of medical equipment. No television. No magazines.

Definitely nothing I could use as a weapon.

"Ugh, I have to get out of here." I was going to go crazy locked in this room when I should be out there helping them find Matthias.

What if he was hurt somewhere and needed me? He'd been completely out of control before, definitely not in his right mind. What the hell was Noah thinking keeping me locked up while they all sat around twiddling their thumbs? Didn't they want to find their friend?

"Hello! Open up!" I banged my fist against the metal door. The sound was obnoxious to my own ears, so I could only imagine how it sounded carrying through the rest of the penthouse.

After a few minutes, I got tired and pressed my face against the glass square in the door. Wait, what was that? Movement? I started banging again until Noah's distinctive frame appeared at the end of the hallway. Silhouetted in the shadows, he looked like some kind of dark angel come to take me to either heaven or hell. Probably hell.

Too late. I'm already there.

"Open up!" Before I could hit my fist against the metal door again, Noah pressed his palm to the scanner and the lock clicked open. He pushed the door open so fast, I had to jump out of the way to avoid getting clocked in the face.

"What the hell is the problem now? People are trying to sleep. Some of us got stabbed tonight." He looked down pointedly at where his T-shirt bulged from the bandages underneath.

Guilt crawled beneath my skin. People sometimes got hurt in the course of carrying out missions. This was an unfortunate side effect of working as an agent. But I'd never allowed that to influence my decision-making. To do this job effectively, you had to be logical, tactical, and efficient. There was no room in that mix for guilt or regret, so it was an uncomfortable and unfamiliar emotion for me in the first place. However, there was no way I could view this job like any other.

It was Matt. My Matthias out there, hurt and alone and possibly getting himself into even worse trouble. Did he know the Family was after him? Oh hell… maybe that was the real reason he'd left. To draw the trouble away from his friends and take it all on alone. That was exactly the kind of thing he'd do. The selfless young man who'd once risked his life to get me to safety was still in there, no matter what Matthias believed.

"I know you don't want to hear this from me, but I am sorry. For the way things went down tonight. For everything. But Matthias is out there, and I can't just sit here while he might need my help. What if he gets hurt while we're waiting around? Can you live with that? With knowing that we were wasting time when he needed us?"

Noah's eyes bored into mine with such intensity I felt like he was examining my brain waves. Jeez, these guys were all intense. And that was saying something since I didn't exactly hang out with choirboys.

"Hold on." Noah let the door close again and walked back down the hall.

I watched until I couldn't see him anymore and then went back to pacing the room. Finally, I sat on the edge of the bed. About five minutes later, Noah came back.

He held out my phone. I took it tentatively.

"Call the Family. Tell them you completed your mission, but the target is in the wind." He paused. "Keep it on speaker."

Of course. Because it wasn't like he trusted me or anything. "I'm not sure how they're going to react. If I don't deliver Matthias to them, they're going to hurt my friend."

Noah regarded me with dispassionate eyes. "It's your job to convince them not to do that. ORUS agents are skilled negotiators. Believe me, I know."

I heaved a sigh but hit the button to call my contact. The same robotic voice answered.

"You have the target?"

I glanced over at Noah as I replied. "I delivered the message to the target. He became violent. There was no way to subdue him."

There was a pause. "Where is the target now?"

"No one knows. He's off-grid."

"This is a mission failure."

I bit my lip. "I was sent in with incomplete information. Target was highly skilled and would have been impossible for anyone to subdue. I can track him, but I need more time."

"Time is of the essence."

"I understand. That's why I've been tracking him the past few hours," I lied. "He's heading west. I should be able to catch up to him if I leave now."

Another pause. "Do not fail again."

"Wait! Where is Sabine? Can I talk to her?"

The line went dead. I almost threw the phone against the wall. Every day that passed, the likelihood that Sabine would be okay diminished. And the fact that they wouldn't allow any contact was a bad sign. What if my friend was already dead? Suddenly it all hit me at once, and I was overwhelmed with fatigue.

The door opened and Rafe walked in. But it was the man who walked in behind him that had me standing at attention.

"Orion. Sir."

Ian stared at me, but I wasn't sure if it was a greeting or a warning. No doubt, he wasn't happy with how much I'd already revealed about my mission.

I nodded at him and then glanced at Noah.

"Ian is willing to work with us. We both agree that having a possibly unstable Matthias out there in the world is a bad idea."

"So what do we do?" I asked. Clearly Noah wasn't going to allow me to track Matthias on my own, not that I even could. He wasn't the typical target.

"An agent just reported that a plane is missing from one of our hangars. We now have a rogue ex-ORUS agent on a plane to Canada." Ian's expression was full of piss and vinegar.

Noah seemed surprisingly calm about it. When he noticed my stare, he shrugged. "It's Matthias. I figured he would be out of the country by now. We're lucky he only went to Canada."

"What's in Canada?" Rafe asked.

"Hell if I know," Noah replied. "But you can bet your ass that if Matthias went there, it's for a reason. So we follow."

———

Matthias

I HIKED my backpack higher on my shoulder and jumped over a fallen log. I'd been on the move for an hour and had just passed the landmark for the halfway point to my cabin.

I'd originally bought the place with no intentions of keeping it as a safe house. It was too close to the United States and ideally, I'd have preferred a warmer climate than Canada. But once I'd seen it in person, I'd decided to keep it. Something about the stark landscape and simple, rustic nature of the place called to me. And I was damn glad I'd kept it now. After what I'd been through over the past twelve hours, I wasn't sure I could have handled a long flight to some far-flung country.

What did happen back there? Now that I was on the move and the imminent danger had passed, I could allow myself to relax enough to reflect. Although maybe I just hadn't wanted to think of it before now. The flashes of memory were more than enough to turn my stomach.

You tried to hurt Gemma.

I shook my head, unable to deal with that part first. Maybe once I wrapped my head around the idea that I'd attacked my friends, I could go there. But I'd fought like a cornered animal. I'd stabbed Noah. My chest burned with shame and also worry. Was he okay? Would anyone even attempt to let me know if he wasn't? I didn't blame them if they'd already cut off all thoughts of me. It was my worst nightmare come true.

I truly was a danger to everyone I loved.

That depressing thought stayed with me as I hiked

the next two miles. The cabin came into view between the trees and I sped up, eager to check things out and start securing the place. I didn't plan to be there long, just until I could arrange my next stop. I'd just been anxious to get out of New York. Noah had too many contacts there, and it would have been nearly impossible to hide even when I was operating at my top form.

Which I clearly wasn't.

I bypassed the front door and went directly to the shed in the back. Inside, there was a small lockbox that appeared to be for tools. I keyed in the combination and then slid out the drawer. An old-fashioned silver key was nestled amongst a bunch of tools. Even though I'd had electronic locks installed on all of the cabin's exterior doors, I liked to keep things old school and used manual locks as well.

I smiled at what Rafe would say to hear me call a metal lock 'old school.' Then my smile fell when I remembered that Rafe was likely going to kill me the next time we met up. My life was no longer my own. My friends were no longer my friends.

I was on my own.

Determined not to get distracted, I palmed the key and walked back out of the shed, my boots crunching through the snow as I crossed to the back door. I entered the electronic code and then used the key to unlock the deadbolt. As soon as I entered, I could tell that the woman I'd hired to look after the place had done her job. It smelled clean, and there were bags on the kitchen counter. When I'd sent her the message that I was on my way, I hadn't been sure she'd get it in time to stock the place.

I shucked off my heavy coat and boots, leaving them in a heap by the door. First thing, I headed to the refrigerator and found some bottled water. After guzzling the whole thing, I stood staring out of the window into the backyard.

What the fuck was I supposed to do now?

This wasn't like me. I always had a plan. But then again, I'd always had control of my own mind. Clearly, I wasn't the one in control now. I had no idea what had happened back at the penthouse other than I'd suddenly been filled with rage and attacked my friends.

And Gemma. Don't forget her.

I hung my head then walked down the dark hallway that led to the single bedroom. A heavy blue comforter was on the bed, and the light on the nightstand was on. A simple kindness but it gave me the sudden urge to cry. How long since anyone had thought to leave a light on for me? To care if I was in the dark? The only person who'd ever gone to bat for me was Noah, and I'd repaid that kindness with a knife.

I winced as pain lanced through my temples again. I'd had these random pains off and on for the past few hours, and each time it had been so sharp I'd feared I would pass out. The first time had been while running away from the penthouse. I'd almost gotten hit by a cab. It had been a godsend that I'd had the plane on autopilot when it happened the second time.

I curled up on top of the comforter, tucking my hands beneath my chin like a child. Sleep snatched me quickly, and I was back at the scene of the crime, watching it all happen again.

"No. Please no," I muttered. Part of me was aware I was dreaming, but I still couldn't wake up.

Then the scene switched, and it was the day before. I was with Gemma and she was smiling at me in that way that made me feel like I could do anything. She grabbed my hand and held it to her cheek. She was so soft.

I dipped my head and kissed her, the brush of her tongue against mine igniting a ferocious need. My hands tunneled into her hair, grasping the long locks like a vise. I was desperate for her, for more of her, and there was an urgency behind it, like I'd better take it all before it was gone. Scared that I was hurting her, I pulled back, but Gemma's fingers dug into my arms, her nails breaking the skin. "No, don't stop. Never stop."

I relished the pain of her holding me so tightly, and

we kissed like we were devouring each other. Lips sliding over skin, hands moving over flesh, we both were ravenous and untamed. The heat built as we fell onto a bed. I couldn't even be sure where we were, and I didn't care. At that moment, the only thing I cared about was that I was in her arms.

"Don't hurt me, Matt!" Gemma's hands clawed at my arms, leaving bright slashes of blood where her nails broke the skin.

I reared back in alarm. In just seconds the scene had gone from dream to nightmare. My hands were wrapped around Gemma's throat, choking her.

"Oh God. I'm so sorry. So sorry, Gemma." I threw myself away from her, and the shock of hitting the floor woke me up. I gasped, taking in huge gulps of air as I surveyed the unfamiliar surroundings. It was dark, save for a soft glow coming from a lamp a few feet away. After a few seconds of disorientation, it all came back. I was at the cabin. Alone.

"Fuck. What have I done?" I grasped my head as the pains returned. But in that moment, I didn't even want to get rid of the pain. I'd take it.

I deserved it.

5

Gemma

To say it was tense on the airplane was an understatement.

Noah and Rafe kept eyeballing Ian. Ian, not one to be cowered, glared back. I mostly just sat at the window and tried not to twitch as my nerves ate at me. Oh no, it wasn't the fact that I was locked into a flying sardine tin with killers who were currently armed to the teeth. Nope, that wasn't it. I was worried about Matthias. I was terrified of what he might do.

I knew him well enough to know he wasn't himself. But there was a part of him that had hesitated with me back there, a part of him that I could still reach. I just had to get close enough. *Yeah, but where is he?*

Matthias was slick. He hadn't left many clues. If Noah and Rafe hadn't been looking for charter flights, they might never have even considered an ORUS plane. Matthias's operation had been so slick Ian hadn't even known a plane was missing until his pilots went to take off for their mission. He'd been that quiet. *Silent.* And the fact that he'd gone so far as not killing anyone spoke volumes.

Yeah, but he doesn't want to get caught.

No. He'd avoided it deliberately. I knew him, even if he didn't know himself. He was capable of love and compassion. I didn't care about what Rafe said, or about what Ian said. Noah, while concerned, was more along the lines of my thinking. He believed in Matthias. He believed that all we had to do was reach him.

I could hear the quiet conversation between Noah and Ian. Rafe was still glaring at Ian as if he wanted to cut the other man's throat out, but Noah was at least getting on with it and focusing on the task at hand. "Okay, so I have Max meeting us at the airstrip. If anyone can get to Matthias, it'll be him."

Ian sat back. "So now you're contacting my agents without checking with me first?"

Electric charges skipped between the two. The

corner of Noah's lips ticked up in a slight smirk. "For starters, I know that you're perfectly well aware that Max is meeting us. After all, he's the logical choice. He's an agent, well trained for the field, but also an excellent psychiatrist and I know that Max doesn't believe in deception unless necessary, so he's already called you. And see, if you hadn't approved it, he wouldn't be there because he is still *your* agent, so you can stop the posturing and being pissed off now. I didn't go behind your back. I asked a friend for a favor. Besides, don't you think you owe me by now?"

The muscles in Ian's jaw ticked, and his lips twitched slightly. The thing was, I couldn't be sure if he was pissed or if he wanted to laugh. From what I'd heard, Ian had been the one to recruit Noah, or rather, Noah had saved his life and Ian hadn't returned the favor.

Becoming an agent was one of those gifts or favors one could probably do without. And from all the stories, I knew Noah was responsible for making Ian the new head of ORUS, the new Orion. So their relationship was complicated at best.

Rafe turned on the projector map on the plane and focused in on the areas surrounding the landing strip. The airstrip was just a stone's throw from Toronto.

"Okay, I've mapped all of his likely exit points, given everything we know about him. The problem is the kid has been all over the world. So his hidey-hole could be anywhere, but hiding in the city makes sense. There're lots of exits and easy ways to blend in. And we all know the kid is good at blending. It's easy to get lost in the world right off-the-grid when you're in the city. He obviously has experience living underground and going undetected. He's going to be really difficult to find. Noah, you know him best. What is his favorite city? I think we all know that Toronto is just a jumping-off point."

I wasn't sure I agreed with that. I spoke up tentatively. "Actually, all Matthias ever wanted when we were kids was to get back to his gran. I know I've been gone for a while now, but I think he'd go somewhere quiet. I also think he doesn't want to hurt anyone, so very likely he'd sequester himself somewhere far away from people where nothing would be able to trigger him. The city is too dangerous for everyone around him.

"The chaos, the noise... I honestly doubt he's going to head straight to another city right away. You saw him. Something triggered that, breaking him. And even though he hurt Noah, you saw the look on his face. He was torn up. He wouldn't want to do that to anyone else."

I stood up and walked to the map. "I think a wooded

area is the first place to look for him. Like an isolated cabin or something."

Ian pondered for a moment before speaking. "Well, we could get another team up here, do a sweep outside the city and look for evidence that he's gone to ground. I mean, it is Canada. It will take a while to get to the woods. It would be easy to get lost."

Rafe shook his head. "Look, I get what you're trying to say, but experience has taught us well. Every ORUS agent has a number of safe houses. They're all designed to be in the city with easy access to weapons and backup. That will be his first move until he's had enough time and distance to set up identities, passports, and people that will help him find a way out."

I shook my head. "I'm telling you, he's not himself. I don't think he's going to settle in to his training. That's what he would do if he was in his right mind, which stabbing Noah clearly indicates he's not." I nodded toward the map again. "If I were him, I'd be in the woods." I pointed to the most likely area. "Not too far in because he'll want access to weapons. And let's face it, it's Matthias, so he'll want internet access. I'd suggest this area to start."

Noah studied us all. His shrewd gaze settled on each of us, assessing what we'd said. Finally, he said, "Ian, get a team up here. We'll chase on this potential lead, but in the meantime, we stick to the plan assuming he's going off his trail. Only then, the doc might be able to tell us more."

I knew it was Noah's show. After all, thanks to whatever I'd done, he'd been stabbed. But I knew they were wrong, all of them. And they were going to waste valuable time in getting to Matthias.

MATTHIAS

MY EYES POPPED OPEN.

Something was wrong. Slowly, I reached under my pillow for the smooth handle of my knife. On the bedside table sat my gun. I strained to listen, but I heard nothing. It was quiet. Too quiet. As if someone had shrouded my cabin in a sound barrier. It was never this quiet.

Birds, animals—they liked to talk at night, so something was disturbing them, scaring them, making them be quiet. Slowly, I shifted out of bed, weapons at the ready. Someone was here. The question was were they friend or foe?

Well, let's not wait and find out, shall we? It was dark

inside my bedroom, except for the alarm clock. It was a new moon tonight, so there was no light. It meant I'd need my night vision.

Or, you're overreacting because normal people don't think about night vision goggles.

Though, normal was overrated Even as I deftly avoided the loose board in the floor that always creaked, I strapped my knife to my leg. Maybe I *was* overreacting, but I'd been well trained for a reason. It had kept me alive for years. So I'd just go ahead and listen to the hairy eyeball instinct that was basically trashing the hotel room of my brain right now.

Something was off. I could feel it. The hairs on the back of my neck were telling me something was out there. *Someone* was out there.

And then the light on my alarm clock flickered. What the hell? Okay, someone was here, and they were fucking with my electrical grid. Considering that I had solar panels and a generator, that shouldn't happen.

So it was going to be like that? I could take it. Quickly, I tossed on a long-sleeved shirt and jammed my feet into my tennis shoes. Under my pajamas, I strapped another knife to my ankle. As much as I enjoyed knives, they were close combat tools. For unwelcome intruders, I'd need guns. They were faster.

And simple rule of thumb was that you didn't play

with your food, unless you had endless amounts of time. And as I didn't know how many people were here for me, now was not the time for playing. Now was the time for getting shit done.

I palmed the piece on the bedside table. Over the doorframe, I silently grabbed my TAC-338A rifle and set it on my shoulder. My second piece was already on the waistband of my pajama bottoms. That would cover me if the trouble was closer than expected. Long range and short-range capabilities would do the trick. At least until I knew the lay of the land.

I opened my door as silently as I could. The average person wouldn't have heard the door. But if ORUS, Blake Security, or the Family were here, they would have *felt* that. A subtle shift in the energy of the air, and they would know I was coming.

Fair enough. Let them know. They'd made the mistake of coming after me, so it wasn't going to end well for whoever it was.

On the balls of my feet, I silently treaded down the hallway. On the other side of that door was a wall covering the length of the hallway, which was perfect for situations like this when I needed a moment to decipher what I was dealing with. I went left toward the front of the house. From that vantage point, with my night scope on and the large open windows, I could see clear into my front yard. I could see who was coming for me. I could see who was out there.

As I walked, it was still way too silent. Was it Rafe? Had he come after me for what I did to Noah? I only remembered hitting him in the shoulder, but my memories weren't reliable. Had I stabbed him more than once? My gut soured and cramped at the thought of my friend being gone.

You did that. Deal with it.

Or maybe it wasn't Rafe. Maybe ORUS had come after me in retaliation? Maybe they'd decided I was too dangerous? They'd come to put me down and all that, or to take me alive and force me back in.

Yeah, they could feel free to piss off. That would be a fight to the death. There was no way in hell they were taking me alive.

The other option was the Family, though they weren't as well trained as ORUS, and definitely not as well as Blake Security. Unless they had contracted out. If they'd gone the hired assassin route, I had no idea what was waiting on the other side. It was likely they'd want me alive so they could torture me first, because that's how they rolled.

Yeah, real nice blokes.

At the end of the hallway, with my night scope on, I saw nothing though. Not a thing. No car, no evidence of someone outside—nothing was disturbed. I pressed the button at the side of the goggles that gave me heat signatures. Save what looked like maybe a deer and a couple of smaller animals, maybe squirrels, there was nothing.

Or are you hiding from the ghost of your past? Maybe there was nothing to be afraid of. Maybe there was nothing out there.

No. My instincts were screaming. Something was wrong.

Or are they in the house already?

Motherfucker. My head had been so fucked up since a couple of days ago. Was it possible I'd slept through the original breach?

No, you're better trained than that.

Yeah, I *was* better trained than that, but I also knew better than to attack my best friend. The one man who had given me family, who had shown me real love.

Yeah, you knew better, but you still did it. You are not in control right now.

Fuck. And if I wasn't in control, that meant I might have woken up late. The danger was already *in* the house. Quickly, I spun and adjusted my footing to bring me back toward the rear of the house, the kitchen, the dining room, and the living room. As I approached the end of the hallway, my heart beat a hundred miles an hour. The *thud, thud, thud* sounded like a cannon in my ears. Had I fucked up?

There's no point crying about it now. Get on with it, mate. Waste these motherfuckers and then we can get on with another day.

As I tiptoed into the kitchen, I frowned. There was no one in the dining room. No one in the kitchen, which only left… I rounded the corner and sure enough, there were the heat signatures I was looking for. Two of them in the middle of my living room. They smelled familiar. Quickly, I tapped the button at the side of my goggles again. Damn it, the night vision didn't allow me to see enough.

I pressed the button on the side of the goggles once more, bringing my vision to normal. I snapped my fingers twice. And that brought the lights up, naturally dimmed to reading level.

Yeah, I had a clapper, so what? I'd always wanted one when I was a kid. I remembered seeing those commercials when I'd been at my gran's on those late night shows she'd like to watch.

The moment the lights flickered on, I knew. I knew why it had been so silent. A ghost and a shadow were in my cabin. And the ghost had a knife to the shadow's throat. I didn't even think. I just reacted. I fired a shot. It went right by Rafe's right ear. Rafe's eyes went wide as he jerked Gemma to my left.

Then I was on the move. I didn't think. I didn't blink. I just had to get her away from him. I learned once, long ago, just how fast Rafe de Marco was. And from that point on, I'd been working to make myself faster, better, stronger.

Rafe had more experience on his side, but I was deadlier. Rafe had no choice but to let Gemma go as I went for him.

I let the pent-up irritation and anger from the last couple of years flow through my veins. And now I was letting it all out. Fists, elbows, knees. We traded them back and forth. All the while, Gemma said nothing. She just kept the hell out of the way. Rafe blocked most of my hits, but then I got a good, clean jab to the face. His head snapped back, and his curse was low. "Motherfucker."

And then he came for me.

A fist landed in my gut. I'd seen it coming. I had tightened my muscles, but fuck all, Rafe could deliver a punch. I countered it with an uppercut, and he staggered back but stayed on his feet.

Kicks, punches, more elbows. I had the perfect elbow number two lined up, but Rafe blocked it. I countered and then we were rolling right to the ground.

Enough was enough. I was done fucking around. I was going to put this motherfucker in the grave now. I reached for the gun in my waistband, and Gemma screamed at me, "Matthias, no."

Rafe put his hands up. The weird thing was the fucker was barely breathing hard. My finger twitched on the trigger.

Rafe's expression was half snarl, half grin. "Do you feel better now that you've gotten that out of your system?"

I blinked at him. "What the fuck are you on about? Shut up and get on your knees."

Gemma's voice was soft. "Matthias, listen to me. We're not here to hurt you. *Rafe* isn't here to hurt you."

I could hear her voice, and it sounded soothing and believable. But Rafe had had a knife to her neck. I'd had to help her, even though she was a liar. Even though she'd hurt me. I had to help her. I had to.

"Noah, Doc, Ian, come on out."

Noah?

What the fuck? The sliding glass door opened, and three men walked in. I scooted back, keeping the gun pointed at Rafe. Two of the people were familiar to me. The other one, I didn't know.

Noah held his hands up. "Listen to me, kid. You don't want to do that."

I shook my head. "Nah, mate, you're dead. I killed you. Didn't I? I stabbed you myself."

Noah smirked. "Rumors of my demise have been greatly exaggerated. You know I'm a tough bastard to kill."

"No, you're dead. You're dead." The memories were swirling in my head, and I couldn't tell what was real.

Next to me, Rafe spoke, his voice low, soothing. "Yeah, you did stab him. But I get the impression you weren't yourself. You're not the only one in the penthouse who knows how to provide medical care. And at the end of the day, I don't think you really wanted to kill him. You barely stabbed the guy. You didn't go very deep. I had the doc come by and stitch him up. He's in pain. I mean, there's a reason why he wasn't in here mixing it up with you, but he's fine. Look at him."

I shook my head. "No, you're fucking with my head... the lot of you. And who the fuck is that?"

Gemma spoke, slowly approaching me, and her voice was soothing. "He's a doctor. I think something I said to you the other day set you off. It's not your fault what happened. And like Rafe said, Noah is fine."

I still didn't believe them.

Ian was here. I knew what Ian wanted from me. To bring me back, to drag me back to the darkness. I wasn't going.

"You're trying to trick me."

The other guy in the room slid a glance to Gemma. "Gemma, say it again."

She frowned. "I don't think I can. I don't know what's going to happen. He has a gun on Rafe."

The doctor repeated again, "Say the line."

And then Gemma said, "From the shadows come the sun."

The pain started in my head again. My finger twitched on the trigger, but I fought it. I kept glancing at Noah and then Gemma, back to Ian, Noah, down at Rafe, back at Noah, and then Gemma. I always went back to Gemma. And as I looked at her, watched her, I wanted to bury the longing I had for her. My finger eased off the trigger.

Before I could think to do anything else, Rafe had my trigger hand twisted around and then applied just the right amount of pressure to my wrist to force me to drop the gun.

"I should have killed you when I had the chance."

Rafe just smiled. "It's good to have you back, kid." And then he popped me in the face. "That'll teach you to respect your elders."

———

Matthias

"HOW ARE YOU FEELING, MATTHIAS?"

"Like shit, mate. How the fuck do you think I feel?"

I glared at Max. Noah had spoken about the shrink before, but I'd never met him. I always wondered how a doctor dedicated to do no harm could do work for an organization like ORUS.

ORUS isn't the same place it was.

The doctor nodded. "I imagine this all feels very disorienting. What was the last thing you remember about the penthouse?"

I braced myself. "Not much." I wasn't looking forward to the onslaught of pain between my eyeballs.

The doctor inclined his head. He narrowed his eyes slightly as if to give me warning that he wasn't going to let me off the hook. I was going to have to talk about this. And then the doc sat back, folded his arms, and waited.

I rolled my shoulders. "Fine. I remember stabbing Noah. I remember the way his blood felt on my hands. I remember watching the pain, the horror, and not being able to do a damn thing about it. So if you're asking if someone took over my body or something, you're barking up the wrong tree, bruv. I'm not possessed just a psychopath."

The doc nodded and wrote something down then shifted his gaze back to me. "So, you feel remorse?"

I glared at him. What the fuck kind of doctor was he? "Of course, I feel remorse. Noah, he's more than my mate. He's my bloody brother, and I was able to do something like that to him. He trusted me with his family, his wife, his baby, and I literally stabbed him in the bloody back, mate. Well, the shoulder. Of course, I feel remorse."

The doctor just nodded. The corners of his lips shifted as if listening patiently to a child having a tantrum. I sat back, my jaw clenching and then grinding. That was when the doctor spoke.

"If you were a psychopath, you wouldn't feel remorse. You wouldn't feel anything, at least nothing beyond your own desires." He studied his notes again briefly and then asked, "Tell me how you feel about Gemma."

Oh hell no. "I feel like a bloody wanker for believing her. There's a part of me that might hate her."

"Is that why you tried to kill Rafe earlier?"

I frowned. I examined the round of emotions from earlier. Rafe holding a knife to Gemma's neck, and the rage that flooded through me. I shook my head to clear it. "I don't know what that was. She lied to me and pretended to be something she wasn't. I don't feel anything."

Max nodded and then flipped back through his notes before pinning me with a stare. "I'm going to read back the events of earlier to you, and then you tell me if that sounds like a man who doesn't care."

The doc's notes were surprisingly accurate. I felt like I'd been a rat in a cage conforming to exactly how I'd been expected to perform. Move by move, blow-by-blow, punch for punch. *You've been a pawn.* As the doc spoke, the rage boiled under my skin.

Why couldn't they just leave me alone? I'd left to protect them. And now they'd interrupted my solitude.

"While you're reading – yeah, okay fine, maybe I didn't want Rafe to hurt her. I know what he's capable of. And fine, I'm angry with her, but I don't want any more bloodshed."

The doctor nodded and held up his hand as if they were going to respectfully disagree on that. "Why don't you tell me why you left?"

I blinked. "Are you *mad*? I'm a danger to everyone. I had to get out of there. Lucia, JJ, Izzy, they were all in danger from me. Everyone was in danger from me. I already proved that with what I did to Noah."

"When you woke up that day, was it your intention to kill Noah?"

"No. Are you fucking listening, mate? I don't know what happened. The monster I keep chained up got loose, and some bad shit went down. So I left to bloody get away from everyone before it happened again."

Max nodded. "So, you came in with Gemma, and after discovering who she worked for, you sat down with Rafe and Noah. You were angry, but you didn't hurt Gemma."

I shook my head. "I don't *want* to be violent." I glanced at him and curled my shaking hands into fists. I didn't want to show the weakness. I didn't want to show how I was feeling. I didn't want to let the emotion out. A part of me feared what that emotion would do.

Will anyone else get hurt because of me?

"I thought I would never hurt any of them. They're the only family I've ever had. Real family. I don't know what happened. I couldn't guarantee it wouldn't happen again, so I left."

"So you came in ready to let Noah handle Gemma and the situation, but somehow you left scared. What changed? What happened?"

I frowned. I gently probed the corners of my brain to see if it would still be intact if I tried to think about that one-minute span at the penthouse where my whole life had changed. I poked at the Gemma memories. The ones where I was wrapped around her, her warmth seeping into my body, making me feel safe and happy. Those wounds were fine.

Then I probed the last happy memory of sweeping her hair off her neck before seeing that cluster of dots that was her call-sign tattoo. The anger welled, but there was no pain left in that memory. Piece by piece, I walked through the events of that morning, right up until the sit down with Noah and Rafe. I was able to probe until the point where Gemma gave excuses, and she was pleading with me, and then—

Pain.

I could feel it between my eyes, rapidly spreading through my whole head, exploding and radiating to my extremities, crippling me, making me curl up into a ball.

In the distance, I could hear rushing footsteps, shouting, and arguing.

The one thing that permeated the ball of pain was the doctor's calm voice. "You have to let this happen."

And then Gemma. "He's in pain. Can't you see? *What did you do to him?*"

"It's not what *I* did to him. Someone planted a code in his head. Neuro-Linguistic programming, along with something else. When I examine a specific memory, this happens."

I tried to pull my brain in focus. Pain. God, the pain. I couldn't control it. I couldn't master it. All I wanted to do was die. I was vulnerable, too vulnerable. *Exposed*. I didn't even have my weapons.

I heard Noah's voice. "Doc. We need to do something."

"Oh, we will. Now that I've confirmed my suspicions, I can help. But right now, he has to ride that wave through the pain. There's nothing I can do about that. In the meantime, Gemma, say the phrase again."

Gemma's voice was soft. "But it's hurting him. I'm the cause of his pain."

Max's voice was the one I could hear the most. "No, someone else did this to him. I suspect it was a long time ago. They just used you to trigger it and take him over."

The last voice I heard to avoid the pain was Noah's. "Is there a way to undo this? Undo what they did to him?"

"Yes. But I suspect it's going to be more painful than anything. *He* didn't stab you. Someone programmed him to annihilate everything in his path. Because he knows that all of you are family, it's the only reason that everyone is still standing. It's because he's so strong that Noah walked away with only a shoulder wound. Someone wanted him to be dangerous. Someone wanted him to be a soldier... a soldier for them. They triggered him. But Matthias was stronger than they thought. He resisted."

As the edges of my vision went gray, I struggled to focus on what they were saying, but I couldn't understand it. The doc was saying I wasn't a monster. Someone had made me this way. The last thought I held on to as the darkness washed over me was that there might be hope for me.

6

Gemma

HE WAS BACK. It had been two days of everyone watching him warily and several sessions with Max. But I could see it. He was back.

I hated to think that I didn't have any faith left, but after everything that had happened, I hadn't been sure I'd ever see the real Matthias again. But now as he gazed down at me like the sun, the stars and the moon were all reflected in my eyes, I could feel it. My Matthias was back, the one who only showed his true self to me.

"I was so scared," I whispered.

Somehow, he understood exactly what I meant.

Matthias pulled me closer until I was right under his arm, nestled against his chest.

"We're going to figure this out. Doc and the guys seem to know more about this than I do. And they believe that we can undo the programming." He sounded annoyed at the idea that someone else could know more about a subject than he could.

I smiled at that. My super genius and his ego.

"I'm here every step of the way," I whispered and cuddled closer, unashamed about needing to be near him right now.

Taking a nap in the middle of the day had become a necessity for him to help manage the pain of the headaches. I had spent an embarrassing amount of time just watching him sleep, grateful beyond all measure that he was okay and consumed by guilt that I had inadvertently caused this.

Had the Family known the extent of the destruction they'd unleashed? They'd sent me in completely unprepared, and for what? What value did an unhinged Matthias have to them? Or maybe that was the wrong assumption. Maybe they didn't need him to have value.

They needed him to be eliminated.

What better way to take care of an enemy than to make him a danger to himself and those around him? They'd probably figured that ORUS or one of Noah's team would take him out for being a threat. But they'd forgotten to consider one part of the equation. Something the Family couldn't possibly understand.

Love.

Matthias was surrounded now by people who loved him. And they were willing to brave his darkness to keep him in the light.

"I love you," I whispered.

Matthias went still and then looked down at me, his face carefully blank. Then he shuddered and grabbed me so tightly I could barely breathe.

"Say it again," he muttered, the sound muffled against my hair. The shock in his voice filtered through easily though, and there was a waver in his voice, almost like he was ashamed at needing to hear it again.

"I love you, Matthias. So much." I hoped that my words could express not just how I felt about him but also that he was *worthy* of it.

His lips pressed against my hair and then against my temple. "I was so afraid that you would never look at me the same way again. That every time you saw my face, all you'd see is a monster. Because that's what I am, Gemma. That's what they made me."

I pushed back until he could see my eyes. "I see the monster, but I also see you. The boy who tried to protect me and the man who is trying to save me even now. I see all of that, and I love you still. Nothing can ever change the way I feel."

When our lips met this time, there was nothing hesitant or gentle about it. Matthias shifted until he was lying on top of me, and his lips didn't release mine for so long that I finally had to turn away to gasp for breath. But I clutched him tightly, just as desperate to keep him close. Now that I had him back, I was afraid to let go.

"I may be a monster, but I'm *your* monster. All of this, every broken part, is yours. And I would die before I let anyone hurt you, Gemma. Even me."

It scared me how solemn the declaration was, and I grasped his face between my hands. The energy was practically vibrating off him he was so wound up. I held him still.

"That's the last thing I want. I need you here with me. Promise me."

He hesitated. I sighed. It was frustrating, but I understood why. He was still in the weeds of what had been done to him. No doubt he foresaw a bad ending and wouldn't want to tie me to him. Well, fuck that. I was going to be there for him whether he was ready for it or not.

"Promise me," I demanded again.

His mouth fell open on a pant when I wrapped my legs around his waist. "I promise."

His hips rotated, thrusting his hard length between my legs. I reached down and gently tugged on the cotton shorts he was wearing. The material gave way easily and his hard length fell into my hand. I reveled in the warmth coming from his skin, my thumb brushing gently over the metal on the tip of his erection.

His answering groan was like music and I experimented, tugging gently on the ring before venturing lower to stroke and tease.

"You don't know what that does to me." He gritted out the words before flipping us over, settling me on top.

I hastily pulled the T-shirt I'd slept in over my head and threw it on the floor. Matthias's eyes heated as his gaze landed on my breasts, his fingers going directly to my hard nipples. The brush of his fingertips over the sensitive points made me lose my train of thought, but I was quickly brought back to it when I felt the hard length between us.

"Ride me. I want to see you fall apart. To give you all the pleasure you deserve."

It was still nerve-wracking to be so on display, but it was Matthias and the look in his eyes could convince me to do almost anything. So I rose up, grasping his cock in one hand and guiding it between my legs. I was so wet already that it slipped easily between the lips of my sex. We both gasped at the sensation.

"I don't really know what I'm doing," I began as I rubbed him around in circles.

Matthias chuckled darkly. His eyes were hot on mine as he said, "Oh, I think you know exactly what you're doing to me."

The blatant sexual appreciation in his eyes banished the last of my nerves. I felt like a goddess as I slowly sank down on him until his full length was buried inside. By the time I was done, we were both gasping and Matthias looked crazed. His fingers flexed against my waist, like he was scared to touch me.

"Make love to me, Matthias. I don't want you to hold back. Not with me."

His eyes flared with lust and love. Then I gasped as his fingers tightened around my waist and held me in place as he thrust upward. The motion sent his cock right against my G-spot, and I screamed at the pleasure before I could stop myself. Thank God this cabin was so remote, or we'd have the neighbors calling the police.

Matthias grunted as I finally found my rhythm, rocking against him as he thrust upward until we were moving in sync. He was so hard and filled me just right. Every thrust of his hips brought me closer and closer to unraveling.

"Come with me. I love to watch you let go."

I could see in his eyes that he was on the edge, and it

was so hot that it put me there too. With no warning, I clenched down on him as my orgasm whipped through me. All I could do was hold on as Matthias moaned with me.

———

Matthias

HOURS LATER, I was staring at the ceiling while Gemma snored softly next to me. One hand moved up and down lazily, caressing her hair while she slept. The shiny, black strands slid through my fingers over and over again while I marveled at my good fortune in being there to see it.

Gemma was mine. And nothing would ever take her away.

It should have scared me, the certainty that she was mine. Nothing had ever really belonged to me before, not even my own body. First as a member of the Family and then as part of ORUS, I'd always seen myself as a tool. An extension of something bigger than me. But then again, I'd never had anything I'd truly wanted to keep for myself. Not until now.

Not until Gemma.

I sat up slowly, disentangling myself carefully so as not to wake her. She probably thought I hadn't been aware of all the time she'd spent watching me sleep, but I knew. Waking under her watchful and loving eye had given me something I'd never had before. She was worried about me, and for good reason. But I was determined to take care of her, too. And right now, she needed sleep most of all.

I tiptoed out of the room, leaving the door to the bedroom ajar slightly so I could hear when she woke up. The soft light filtering through the cabin windows had that slightly violet tinge that told me it was dusk. We'd slept the whole day away, and already I was itching to get back to her. It took all of my self-control to ignore the urge to go back in the bedroom and slip beneath the covers. I could hold her close again, breathing her scent and feeling her soft hair against my skin. But that would be counterproductive because it would only make it harder on me later if a tough choice had to be made.

"Hold on to what makes you human," I repeated out loud.

Everything the doc had said made sense in the abstract. The programming gave me certain instinctive reactions but ultimately, I was still in control of things on a conscious level. I had to keep the things that made me want to live in the forefront of my mind. Hold on to the people and the things that made me who I was, not the soldier or the machine.

Although I knew it would probably be for the best if I did leave. Gemma would be hurt, but over time, she'd adjust. Settle down somewhere, be safe and happy. Eventually she'd marry some guy who could give her the normal, stable life she deserved, not a loose cannon who was likely to flip out at any moment and possibly harm her without even realizing it.

If I were a different man, a better man, I could let her go to find that life. But I wasn't, and her fate had been sealed. She was mine and had been since the first moment I'd realized who she was.

It was up to me to be the best version of myself I could be. For her. It was all for her.

Slim arms circled my waist, and I stilled.

"What are you doing out here?" Gemma rested her head on my back, and the warmth of her cheek permeated through until I swore I could feel it in my core.

"Thinking. Wishing."

"My wish already came true," she whispered.

I scoffed at that. "Did you wish that a homicidal maniac would lead you on a wild chase to a secluded cabin in Canada?"

She giggled, and the sound was so unexpected I

almost looked around to see where it had come from. This was a side of her that I always wanted to see. Light-hearted. Happy.

I resolved right then and there to always keep her that way. No matter what it took.

"No. Not exactly," she replied. "But I did wish that I could see you again. That things had worked out differently that day by the river."

"And here we are," I finished.

Gemma nodded, eyes shining. It wasn't often that I thought I was lucky. A fucked-up childhood leading to an even more fucked-up adulthood had pretty much driven home the fact that I wasn't ever going to be one of the lucky ones. The ones with the parents who loved them and baked them cookies and shit.

But maybe, just maybe, we could create our own luck. With Gemma by my side, I could conquer anything, especially if it meant keeping her safe. My past with the Family would come to a head, we'd handle it and then move on. Was it too much to believe that we could have a life after this? Live together, maybe buy a house one day with a fence and a dog?

And even though it was a long shot, I had to believe that this whole thing was going to work out.

7

———

Matthias

By the time the rest of the guys returned to the cabin that afternoon, I was ready. I knew what was coming, and even though the thought of talking about my past with the Family made my stomach churn, I was ready for it.

It was time to put it out there and face it head-on.

"Matthias. You're looking well." Max assessed me with a keen eye, making me feel like I'd just passed a test.

I wondered what the doctor had expected. For me to have a nervous twitch? Be sweating and shaking? Hell, if he hadn't been sure that I was okay the last time, then he never should have left me alone with Gemma!

As if she could sense my unease, Gemma appeared at my side and rested a gentle hand on my arm. The touch had the instant effect of a Valium. I smiled down at her, hoping it didn't look as goofy as it felt. Being around her brought out the lightness and the ease that I hadn't felt in years.

This is who I should have been, I thought absently as Rafe, Noah, and Ian filed in after the doctor and took their places in the small, cramped living room. Seeing all the men close to Gemma was already bringing out my protective urges, triggering the assassin to pull close to the surface. But when I was with Gemma alone, the part of me that I'd thought had died when I was a child woke up from years of slumber. She humanized me and made me remember why life was worth living.

It was like sleepwalking for years only to awaken at the edge of a cliff.

"I feel better, Doc. Although I won't be truly happy until I know those fuckers can't play with my mind again."

Ian looked vaguely uncomfortable, and I had to curb the urge to bare my teeth. How many times had ORUS used similar methods on its assets? Hell, for all I knew, there was some other kind of programming deep in my brain waiting to be unleashed.

"How do I break this thing for good? I don't want anyone messing with my mind." I leaned against the opposite wall since all the seats were taken.

Gemma stood next to me and rested her head on my shoulder.

"That's what we're trying to piece together," Max replied smoothly. "I believe that telling us about your time with the organization might provide some insight."

It was insane, really, that the guy didn't seem surprised by any of this. Impressive actually. I wondered what kind of fucked up things he'd seen that he wouldn't bat an eyelash at the idea of a brainwashed former assassin.

"My time with the organization was my entire childhood. Not by choice." I stopped, unprepared for the flood of emotion that thinking about my childhood brought.

Surviving had always been about moving beyond what had been done to me in the past. Thinking about the things I'd seen and heard while with the Family was counterproductive to building a new life. It could only serve to bring me down. So for years I'd suppressed it all, rarely thinking about my time there. It was almost as if there'd never been a little boy who was loved by his mother more than anything in the world, or a little boy who'd loved a little girl who looked at him like he was her protector.

"It's okay, Matthias. They can't touch you now. And they can't take anything else away from you. Never again." Gemma's soft whisper pulled me back from the edge.

I rested my forehead against hers, drawing strength from her certainty and her calm.

"My mother was a prostitute owned by the Family. I was born there. At the time, I had no idea who my father was."

There was a pause before MAX spoke again. "So, the indoctrination could have occurred at any time. However, I'm going to assume it occurred when you were older since your reaction to it was so strong. How old were you when you escaped?"

"Thirteen. And I didn't escape. I only wish I had." I looked over at Gemma and saw the understanding reflected in her eyes.

How different things would have been if my escape plan had worked. We would have been on the street, but at least we would have been together. I would have never entered ORUS, never been taught about death and pain and blood. The computer skills I had at that age would have been enough to get me work doing things that were definitely illegal but would have paid enough to keep us fed and safe. And maybe we would have had enough money to make it north to my grandmother's house.

To a place that could have been a real home.

"At thirteen I attempted to run, but I was caught. I was sold to ORUS shortly after that, so the programming must have taken place before then."

The doctor was taking notes but paused briefly to glance over at Ian. What was that about?

Rafe crossed his arms. "I kept a lot of the case files I worked on when I was active with ORUS. The shit I've seen on the Family was enough to turn my stomach. Nasty business. And the head of the syndicate, the one you call Father, is known for being ruthless and vindictive. I'm not sure what you could have done that would get you on his shit list though. I'm sure plenty of others ran."

"They did. None made it very far. Most of them were beaten. Some were killed."

Rafe narrowed his eyes. "But you were sold to ORUS."

"I was too valuable to waste. They knew I was highly skilled as a hacker. Someone like that would fetch a good price. Plus, it probably amused him to know that a highly trained assassin would essentially be his robot with the right code words."

Gemma folded her arms around herself. I pulled her closer. "Not your fault," I whispered in her ear. But the tension in her body remained.

"But still, what could you have done that warranted being sent out of his control in the first place?" Noah's brow furrowed as he stared at me with the no-bullshit look I'd seen plenty over the years.

"I tried to save a girl." I glanced down at Gemma and then raised my eyebrows.

Identical expressions of understanding crossed Noah and Rafe's faces. From the things I'd told them already about my past with her, I'd known they would get it. I wasn't sure how much Gemma had revealed about her past to Ian or whether I'd be exposing her. But when I looked down at her, she shrugged and smiled softly.

"If we're going to tell it, let's tell it all. No more hiding. No more secrets."

I kissed the side of her head. "It was Gemma. She was brought in to the Family at a young age as collateral on a debt her father owed. I tried to protect her as much as I could, but when I overheard them talking about selling her, I knew we had to get out. There wasn't much I could do on such short notice, but I got her to pack a few things and figured we had better odds of surviving on the street."

Gemma took over. "All I took were my favorite books and my stuffed Tigger. Not the most practical survival kit in retrospect."

To my surprise, Rafe let out a hearty laugh. "At least that explains the Tigger toy in his room. I was getting worried about the kid. Oskar was convinced he had some weird stuffed animal fetish."

I wasn't sure if I wanted to get my knives out or join in the laughter. But even Gemma's shoulders were shaking. If it amused her, I supposed I could stand being the butt of the joke.

"Right. I think Oskar should pay attention to his own problems."

Rafe tipped his chin. "Believe me, I know. I'm the one who's been partnered with him the most. Somebody else should have to put up with his shit occasionally."

"Anyway," I drawled, more than ready to get them back to the matter at hand, "when they caught us, they threw her in the Thames to teach me a lesson. For years, I assumed she'd drowned."

"And I thought he was dead," Gemma added. "That they'd killed him as punishment for trying to save me."

The guilt was apparent in her voice. How fucked was this whole situation? We'd both lived with guilt thinking we had caused each other's death. But in reality, we'd both survived and grown stronger only to find each other again.

Maybe karma wasn't always a bitch.

"So, in answer to your question," I continued, "I was originally on their shit list because I tried to save a girl. But it turns out she didn't need saving anyway."

I kissed Gemma on the neck, relishing the way she cuddled into my embrace. My next words were for her alone.

"She grew up to be a badass all on her own."

Rafe nodded. "That explains why he hated you then. But that doesn't explain why they waited all these years to come after you."

That was when I scrubbed a hand down my face, the weariness taking a toll. "No. It doesn't. But maybe the fact that I've been disrupting their business practices for the last two years does."

Rafe shook his head and then muttered, "Yep, that would do it."

Gemma

After so many heavy revelations, I should have been exhausted. But after Noah and the guys left, I found myself wound tighter than a spring. They'd wanted to dig into the specifics of what Matthias had done, but the doc forced us to take a break. Then he'd spent the rest of the day with Matthias in the woods hiking, talking, and doing whatever it was that he did to deprogram people.

Matthias snored softly next to me, and I turned my head to watch him. It was so good to see him like this, vulnerable and at peace. I suspected this was a side that very few people got to see. Matthias seemed like the type to sleep with a knife under his pillow, not that I blamed him, and yet he was resting next to me comfortably. He had to be exhausted after that dump session with the guys.

"You're so strong. For everyone. But this time, I'm going to take care of you," I whispered. He slept on unaware.

I sighed. I had no idea how we were going to work this situation out. I'd probably signed Sabine's death warrant once Father realized that I'd been compromised. I squeezed my eyes shut against the guilt that brought tears to my eyes.

"I'm so sorry, Sabine."

But I didn't truly think my friend would want me to compromise the safety of others on her behalf. It was an impossible position to be in. How did you weigh the value of one life over another? I couldn't allow the Family to take their revenge on Matthias, not even to save my friend.

But knowing that I had no other choice didn't keep it from hurting so damn bad.

Matthias snorted softly, and when his eyes opened, he stiffened immediately. "Hey, why are you up? Is everything okay?"

"I'm fine. Just couldn't sleep." I soothed him with a gentle caress to his bare arm and he relaxed immediately.

I snuggled down under the covers and Matthias snagged me around the waist and dragged me closer. His warmth against my back was like a balm to my ragged soul. *Love can do that*, I thought. It could heal the things that were broken inside you. Something I'd never believed before.

"I'm sorry you had to hear all that earlier," he mumbled against my back.

It took a second for his words to sink in but when they did, I rolled over to face him. Even in the dim room I could see the anguish in his eyes. Matthias was hard to read... even for people who'd known him for a long time, I'd bet. It gave me a small thrill to think that this was something I had of him that no one else did. That perhaps I could see into his soul through all the layers of protection and distrust.

"Why would you be sorry? You did the best you could in that situation. We both did."

"Yeah, but you were out there alone. If I'd known you were alive, I would have never stopped searching for you."

Matthias's eyes locked on my face, his expression grave. I had no doubt that he meant that quite literally. He didn't let many people in, but the ones he did earned undying loyalty. Something inside me blossomed at the knowledge that I was loved like that. Completely and wholly.

I moved closer, pressing my face against his neck. "There was nothing you could have done. And I got lucky, actually. Andromeda isn't your typical mother figure, but she loved and protected me. She made sure that no one could ever hurt me again and that I could protect myself. I was lucky."

Matthias smiled. I could feel his lips move against my forehead. "Tell me about her. I have to admit I'm curious about what it would be like to be raised by an ORUS agent. You always speak of her so fondly."

"That's because she didn't treat me like an asset. I'm her daughter. Truly. Her partner Christine took care of most of my day-to-day upbringing since Andromeda was often traveling. In the beginning I didn't really understand what she did. But once I was old enough, she started training me on hand-to-hand and weapons. Christine is actually a decent fighter, too. You'd never guess it to look at her. She looks like a typical soccer mom."

Matthias laughed at that. "That'll teach us all to stereotype, huh?"

"Exactly. They gave me stability and so much love. Most of all, I was safe. Which was exactly what I needed. Especially after losing you. It broke me in a way, and they were worried about me for a long time. I'm not sure I could survive that kind of loss again."

His eyes met mine in the dark. "You won't have to. You'll never lose me again. I feel sorry for anyone stupid enough to try to separate us now."

It was the perfect answer when I was feeling suddenly emotional, and I clung to him, not even caring that he could feel the moisture from my tears all over his chest.

"What about you?" I finally asked once the lump in my throat subsided. Although I knew a lot more from listening to him explain it to the others, I wanted to know what his teenage years had been like. Being sold to ORUS... I didn't even want to contemplate the things he'd probably been through, but I needed to know. I had an insatiable desire to know everything about him.

"What about me?" Matthias asked.

I poked him in his rock-hard belly, storing the memory of his shocked laugh to savor later. It was so rare to see real levity from him and I cherished those moments.

"You know what I mean."

He sighed, the sound slicing through me like a knife. "It was hell, but it was also one of the best things that could have happened to me." There was a pause, and I imagined there was a whole host of things he wasn't saying. "But in the end, ORUS made me a weapon. It's ironic really. The Family sold me as a punishment, but in the end, they created a weapon that could be used against them. They probably didn't think I would survive the training."

I burrowed closer, breathing in the comfort of his scent. I remembered the early days of my ORUS training. If I hadn't been prepped for years by Andromeda beforehand, I might not have survived myself. It was brutal and designed to weed out the strong from the weak.

"But you did," I whispered. "You survived. We both did."

"Yes, we did." Matthias anchored a hand in the back

of my hair, his long fingers stroking a slow, drugging caress over my scalp. "Noah looked out for me, mentored me. I'm not even sure why. But he taught me so much that I could work for years and never repay him."

"I don't think he wants you to repay him, Matthias. He's your friend."

"He is. The best mate anyone could ask for. He took me under his wing and found a way to get me out of ORUS without a toe tag. I'll be forever grateful to him."

Moments passed where the only sound was our shared breathing. Things had truly come full circle, for both of us. From a mad dash in the night, to being brought halfway around the world only to be reunited as adults. It was probably time to consider that fate really was on our side.

"Me too," I whispered.

I sat up slightly, and that was when I saw that Matthias wasn't just being quiet. He was fast asleep. Affection took me by the throat so suddenly that my head swam. What if Noah hadn't protected him when he was in ORUS? What if we'd gone through all of this suffering only for one or both of us to have died before we found each other again? It was nothing short of a miracle that we were together at all.

"I'll be forever grateful to him, too."

8
____

Matthias

I WOKE up with the usual panicked alertness. But right away I knew I wasn't alone. I relaxed when I saw Gemma was in bed with me, curled up on her side, looking so peaceful.

I still wondered how the hell she was able to sleep with me. And then I remembered everything the doc had said. *I* wasn't the monster. Someone put the monster inside me and then honed it to a finely tuned weapon while I was with ORUS. And given the depths of my programming, it was a wonder I hadn't killed everyone at the penthouse.

But I was strong. I could beat this.

Gemma rolled over and her smile was immediate. "Matthias, good morning."

Just hearing her soft voice still full of sleep and calling me by my real name made me smile. When I was with her now, it felt like we'd made it out together all those years ago. I could almost believe the years of pain, torment, and torture had never happened.

"Good morning. Did you sleep okay?"

Something flashed behind her eyes and I felt bad for the question, but I didn't take it back. "Yes, I slept fine. I know yesterday was a tough day. How did you sleep?"

I shook my head. "Fine, I think. No dreams." That meant no nightmares either, which was more rest than I'd had in months. "Come on. Enough lazing around; it's time to get to work."

I wanted to hold her and make love to her, but I'd been hanging around long enough. It was time to fight. It was time to go home. It was time to finish what I'd started. I kissed her softly and dragged the sheets off. By the time we were ready and headed out into the great room of the cabin, I found Noah, Rafe, and the doc already up and ready to go.

"How are you feeling, kid?" Noah's voice was steady and unwavering just like always. I didn't detect a single hint of trepidation or constraint in it.

"I'm all right, mate. You know, nothing a little anti-brainwashing can't solve."

Rafe choked down the coffee. "Too soon, man. Too soon."

I shrugged. "Were you the one who had a homicidal killer implanted into your brain? No?"

Rafe shrugged. "Yeah, okay. Good point. You go on ahead and make all the jokes you want."

"Yeah. Thought so." I then turned my attention to Noah. "So how are we going to go after them?"

Gemma wrapped her arms around my waist and said, "Is this really the safest thing that we can do? Take the fight to them? What if there are other things that they've done to him? How wise is this as a course of action?"

The doc shook his head. "I don't know. I'm just on the payroll to get him back to normal." He leveled a gaze at me. "Like I said, you are stronger than what they did to you. After the hypnotherapy, I can only imagine the amount of pain you've been going through to hold that part of you back. But you've managed it just fine for years. It's a risk. At the same time, I think with the work that we've already done, combined with the fact that you're already a fighter, you'll be all right. But that's a decision you need to make."

I covered Gemma's hands with my own. "In that

case, I choose to fight." I pulled Gemma around into my arms and tucked her under my chin. "After what they did to me, what they did to you, and the fact that they're holding your friend, I want their blood— in a totally non-homicidal way of course."

This time Noah coughed, and muttered, "Well, this is one of those times I think a little homicidal nature is okay."

Gemma met my gaze. "I trust you with my life."

The sliding glass door opened, and Ian aggressively stomped his feet on the doormat before stepping in. "If you guys are done with your Kumbaya moment now, I've got us a plane to head back. What are we doing?"

Everyone turned to look at me and I tucked Gemma even closer as I leveled my gaze on Ian. "We're making a plan to go after the fuckers."

Ian nodded. "That's a plan I can get behind."

Noah spoke up. "Unfortunately, we're flying blind right now. We don't know what they know. We don't know if they programmed you to do or say anything else or to send a signal. You said you don't remember much from the penthouse."

I shook my head. "It's foggy at best. I hopscotched through Midtown and lower Manhattan before I went to the flat. I followed the standard ORUS protocol: double back, all the way around. But I didn't have any details.

Every time I tried to remember too closely, I felt like I'd taken an ice pick to my brain. So I could have done anything."

Noah nodded. "Okay. Then in that case, trying to deceive them into thinking that you're still in the wind is risky and probably won't work. We need to go direct. Hit them at home base."

Ian came forward and poured himself a cup of coffee. "The drive to the port is risky. I can give you all the agents I can spare, but if they're ready for us, it'll be a bloodbath."

I looked down at Gemma and squeezed her tighter. "Look, the Family went to a lot of trouble to get me. For years, they'd been holding on to their ace in the hole. The wankers didn't count on the fact that I might fight back. They very likely didn't count on the fact that I would leave ORUS. They sure as hell didn't count on the fact that I would come after them. So let's give them another surprise. Hand me over."

Gemma's head snapped up and she scowled at me. "Over my dead body."

God, I loved her. "Hopefully it won't come to that, love. With enough backup, I say we take the fight to them under the guise of a complete and total peace-offering type of handover. They'll believe I'm sacrificing myself to protect all of you."

Rafe gave me a lopsided smile. "Is this the part where you also add in, 'Then we kill everybody'?"

I nodded. "Yeah, this is the part. They've caused enough pain. It's time they paid for their sins."

"So exactly what were you doing to get even with the Family? I know Max didn't want us getting in to it earlier, but we need to know what we're up against," Ian said.

I grinned. "Well, just a few things. I changed their shipment manifests, so their shipping routes went wrong. I funneled money to pirates to steal their cargo and set their human cargo free. I stole a couple of planes. Oh, and I stole 1.3 billion dollars from them."

Ian just stared at me, blinking, and then he muttered, "Fuck, I wish you still worked for ORUS."

Noah, however, looked completely unsurprised. He just shrugged. Rafe was the one who stared at me. "Are you fucking kidding me?"

I shrugged. "I'm a hacker. I can always find some way to interfere with someone's life. They were killers. And they left me a lot of open backdoors."

Noah's only question was, "Where's all that money?"

I grinned. "I opened up a fund for all the Family's victims. Everyone who was freed and released, I made sure they got a share, access to somewhere safe to go, and money for their families. That sort of thing. Like we do at Blake Security."

Noah nodded. "Yeah, I taught you well, didn't I?"

Emotion welled, and it took all my years of training to hold myself together. Despite all the bad things I'd done, Noah had always carried an underlying belief that I would do the right things. Like I was... good at the core. Something that I hadn't even believed about myself. And here he was again, years later, still being the brother I'd never known I needed. Further proof that blood didn't make you family.

He'd shown me what real family was about.

"Yeah, you definitely did."

Matthias

THAT DANK WAREHOUSE SMELL, *it wrapped around me like a wet shadow, cloying, clinging, and sticking to me so I couldn't shake it off. It held me rooted to the spot, watching the horror play out in front of me because I wasn't strong anymore. I wasn't trained. I was just a kid and I couldn't help but watch in horror as Becca fell before us.*

The scream caught in my throat, the horror manifesting in freezing chills all over my body, bringing out goose bumps. I couldn't drag my eyes away from her. I wanted to tell her not to do it. I wanted to tell her that everything would be okay. I wanted to tell her that I was sorry she'd even been brought into this place. But I couldn't do that. All I could do was watch.

The silence of her fall was probably the worst part. No scream, no crying out. No sounds came out as her body fell through the air. I could only watch her. I'd done nothing to help. I couldn't erase that from my mind.

"She was my favorite. Now what are we supposed to do?"

It was Father and someone else talking. The words filtered into my consciousness as a little boy who had just seen the most horrific thing. I knew what had happened to the girl and where she'd gone. I knew someone would be upset that she'd died, but clearly not this lot.

"I need to find a new replacement, and quick. Round up all the girls between eight and thirteen. We might just send him a sampling. I'll pick one or two. The rest we'll just sell elsewhere."

The rest they'd just sell elsewhere. The rest they'd just sell—

Just like that, I snapped out of it. Eight and thirteen? Jesus bloody Christ. Gigi. I had to get Gigi. Run.

Even though a crowd had started to gather, I found my

way, winding through the people coming to see what happened to that poor girl. I ran in the opposite direction. I had to see Gigi. I had to get Gigi. Quickly, quickly, my legs moved underneath me. I shook off that dank smell that clung to me, that followed everywhere. Maybe I could outrun that. Maybe I could outrun the horror that was waiting for my friend.

Just run. Keep running. One step in front of the other. I had to save her. I had to get to her.

I barged into the room. "Gigi, we have to go."

But this time, they already had her. Her small body wriggled in the hands of the much larger adults. The kind of people that were supposed to protect her, to keep her safe. Just like you.

Just like me. I'd promised to keep her safe, but I hadn't. I'd failed. I'd failed her. Again.

And you'll keep failing her. You're not fast enough.

A hand pressed my chest hard. Someone was yelling at me, shouting at me. A grown-up. Someone who should be on my side, but I was still small and tired. Tired of fighting. More pressure was on my chest. More anger.

It wasn't until my eyelids opened and the darkness surrounded me that I understood. A dream. It had been a dream, reminding me of what had happened. Reminding me of all the ways I'd failed Gigi.

No. Not Gigi. Gemma.

"Matthias! Matthias, Goddamn it, if you're not going to wake up, I'm going to get Noah and Rafe in here."

I groaned and tried to push myself into a sitting position, only to discover that my T-shirt was soaked through. Shit. I reached behind my head and dragged it off before tossing it into the corner.

Gemma's hands were warm and dry against my skin, and I relished her heat. "I was dreaming about that day when we almost escaped. It seemed so real." I told her the events leading up to when I'd come to grab her. All the things I couldn't tell her at the time when she was too young to know.

She shook her head and ran her hands through my hair. "Shh, we're safe now. We've been safe for a very long time. No one is going to hurt us ever again."

I hadn't even realized that I'd made noise until Rafe and Noah came running into the room, guns drawn at the ready. When I lifted my gaze, Noah immediately lowered his weapon. Rafe's gaze went directly to Gemma and asked, "Are you okay?"

She nodded. "Yeah. I'm fine. He had a nightmare."

Noah addressed me directly. "Kid?"

The icy wash of shame splashed into me. I hated that they had to be afraid of what I could do in my sleep. "Yeah, I'm fine. Sorry, I didn't mean to wake anyone. I wasn't aware I was screaming."

Rafe and Noah exchanged glances, but then they both nodded at us and left. I shoved myself out of the bed then padded over to the wardrobe to grab another T-shirt. When I climbed back into bed, Gemma wrapped herself around me. "You don't have to be scared anymore. You're safe. I am safe. All of that was a different lifetime, and you and I are too strong. You heard what the doctor said... after everything they did to you, you were stronger than their programming. We're all right. Okay?"

I wished I could believe her. Were we safe? Would I do something to put her in danger again?

"I can see your wheels spinning. I remember everything that you did for me. I can imagine the kind of guilt you've walked around with all these years. I survived because of you. Because you got me out of there. Because of you, I had a fighting shot. Even though our escape didn't work out the way you planned, the stars were still aligned to save my life that day. Because if you hadn't come back to get me, I would have ended up just like that girl."

I shook my head. "Please don't say that."

"I have to. You have to know. I attribute my whole life to you. I have hope now, thanks to you. I got out. And, so you know, it wasn't your responsibility. You were a kid too."

"I promised to protect you. Fat lot of good I did."

"You were a kid. We were both kids. But now, we're not children anymore. And we can fight back. They will never know what hit them. You and I, brick by brick, are going to dismantle them. Do you understand me?"

Her voice was firm, strong, and completely utterly unwavering. When I turned my gaze to her, I could see the strength in her beautiful eyes. Her resolve. I knew that if I ever turned back, she'd be right there with me. I wanted to be that for her. "What did I do to deserve you?"

"Oh well, you know. You were just you."

I held her close, inhaling the scent of her shampoo. I loved her. Together, we were going to take down the Family and reclaim our lives.

9

Gemma

COMING BACK to New York should have felt like a victory. But for me it was bittersweet. Our time in the cabin had seemed like an oasis outside of time, just the two of us alone for hours on end.

I hadn't wanted it to end.

Just thinking about the hours we'd spent in bed, licking and sucking each other, made my skin hot. It had felt like he wanted to eat me alive, to devour my pleasure until he was sated. But if his appetite was anything like mine it would never happen. I could gorge on him forever and never have enough.

Now we had to go back to the real world and all its problems.

It was going to be strange to stay at the penthouse where so much had happened. But Matthias was determined that I would be protected. Even stepping foot inside to drop off our gear had felt odd. Somehow out of time and space.

"I don't have much," I reminded him as we parked in the lot in front of the hourly motel where my things were stored. The wind blew softly, a white grocery bag dancing over the gravel lot and landing near the front office. There were only two other cars parked nearby, one right in front of the office that I assumed belonged to the manager and a rusted green sedan that looked like it didn't even work.

The owner had been more than happy to hold my room for the month when I'd presented him with a fat stack of bills, so I wasn't concerned about my things being disturbed. Not that I'd left much here anyway, just clothes and toiletries. A little money. Nothing identifiable.

"Good. That'll make it easier for us to get in and out. I don't like being out in the open like this." Matthias scanned the area around the building, on high alert for any sign of trouble.

On the flight back to the States, we'd talked a little

more about his time with the Family and the threat we posed to them. But I still felt there was more to his story, things he was holding back out of fear or worry about scaring me.

Or because he doesn't trust me.

I sighed and got out of the car, looking around with the same diligence as Matthias. Anyone who attacked us would instantly regret it, but I'd rather avoid bringing that kind of attention. Until we'd figured out exactly how we were going to handle the Family and secure Sabine's safety, I couldn't risk any injury. If I was going to pull off a rescue, I needed to be in top form.

After I unlocked the door, Matthias pushed ahead of me into the room. I shook my head as he moved stealthily toward the bathroom door. A few seconds later he came back out looking slightly more relaxed.

"Clear. Let's get you packed up so we can get out of here. Rafe had to get back to the penthouse, so I don't want to stay here too long without backup."

It was a stark reminder since I'd almost forgotten the other man had been trailing us from the airport. Almost. But until things were settled, I'd have to get used to the sensation of being followed. Matthias had determined that I was in greater danger now that I'd joined forces with him. I thought it was a bit soon to determine that. After all, to anyone outside it would just look as though

I was cozying up to my target, exactly as I'd promised to do. There was no way the Family could know that I'd switched loyalties. But Matthias wouldn't be dissuaded.

Working together, we threw the clothes I'd had draped over the bed into my black duffel bag. I never unpacked while on a job; it didn't make sense, as I was rarely in one place for too long anyway.

While stuffing clothes in the bag, my hand encountered the burner phone I used to communicate with the Family. It was low on power. I was surprised it hadn't died while I was gone, actually. Matthias looked over my shoulder as the screen lit up.

"Is that her?" His voice was quiet. Reverent.

I nodded. "Yes. This is Sabine."

I tilted the phone slightly so he could see the photo displayed on the lock screen more clearly. It was a picture of me and Sabine taken when we were just hanging out on the couch after dinner one night. We were both smiling brightly, and Sabine had lipstick on her teeth. I had teased her about not looking perfect for once.

"She's beautiful," Matthias commented. "Then again, she always was. Even when we were kids. We're not going to let her down, Gemma. I promise, we will figure out a way to get her out."

It was uncanny how he seemed to always know what

I was thinking. But despite all the assurances, I didn't feel any better. No matter how careful we were, it was inevitable that I'd have to make some hard choices. If it came down to the wire and I had to save Matthias or Sabine, it would destroy me to have to choose.

When I'd started this journey, everything had seemed so simple. I was willing to do whatever it took, no matter how unethical, to save my friend. But now I couldn't promise to choose Sabine.

I'd already failed her.

"Let's just go." I was glad he didn't say anything else. It was hard enough not to break down. Part of me wanted to throw the stupid phone against the wall and watch it shatter into a million pieces.

But instead, Matthias just watched me in that quiet, intense way of his.

"Not yet." Then he grabbed me and crashed his lips against mine.

Matthias

I LIFTED Gemma into my arms easily, and she giggled. I

loved her laugh. It was so unfiltered. She really should do it more often.

As I kissed her, she locked her legs around me at the ankles and held on to my shoulders tightly. I hissed when her fingernails dug in to my flesh, and my cock throbbed against her heat. Electricity tingled up my spine. Without even trying, she could bring me to the brink. I didn't want to think about how I'd almost lost her. How we'd almost been torn apart.

I wanted to hold on to every moment we had together. She was mine, despite everything that had happened. We were meant to be together and I would do everything in my power to keep her. As my tongue slid over hers, my hands cupped her ass as I moved her against me, rocking her heated core against my cock. I couldn't get enough. Blindly, I sought out the bed but had to settle for pushing her up against the wall.

My hands impatiently shoved aside the fabric of her T-shirt. With a growl, I broke contact with her lips so I could tug it over her head. I heard a rip and couldn't help but smile against her lips.

With a series of wiggles and grunts, I had her jeans off, then picked her up again. When my fingers came into contact with the edge of her panties, I could feel her slick heat and moaned against her lips.

Take. Taste. Come. Now. I had a serious control problem when it came to Gemma. It didn't matter how much I tried to control myself. Once her lips were under mine, it was over. I wasted no time pushing the fabric of her thong aside. I knew her body well enough now to know when I slid my fingers over her it wouldn't take long to have her panting.

Her lips were so slippery and wet. Sliding my tongue into her eager mouth, I coaxed her tongue into a dance with mine. I wanted her begging and pliant in my arms. Wanted her as desperate as I was. The problem was I was going to explode. The head of my dick pulsed, and I understood why my type of piercing was so popular. Right now, I could come just by thinking about sliding into her, thanks to the stimulation. My hands shook, and my legs trembled, I ached for her so bad. Sliding a finger inside her, I was determined to coax her first orgasm from her.

But I didn't give her the press of my fingers that she craved. Instead, I teased her, spreading her juices over her lips, making sure she was soaked. Making sure to drive her crazy.

Wrenching her lips from mine, Gemma shook her head. "Wait."

I heard the command, but it took a moment to register. Slowly, I blinked into focus as my brain came online.

"What's the matter, love?" I asked through a constricted throat.

"Nothing, but you're not distracting me tonight. I had something else in mind."

I watched her carefully but didn't say a word as she unwrapped her legs and slid down my body. My cock twitched in hopeless protest. What was she up to? Every muscle tensed as I waited on her next move. Need made me twitch. The hitch in her voice and the way her pupils dilated made my skin feel too hot. Too tight.

Gemma yanked my shirt over my head with smooth efficiency. The buckle to my jeans came next. When she wrapped delicate fingers around my cock, I cursed. *Shit. Bugger. Fuck.* I had to squeeze my eyes tight against the urge to come.

She pumped me in a slow, deliberate motion, her gaze never leaving mine. When her palm contacted the crown of my cock, grazing my piercing, I shook.

"Gemma—" I barely managed to get the warning out past my clenched teeth.

She licked her lips as her gaze slid over my body to my straining erection. Blood surged to my groin, and I jerked involuntarily in her palm.

"Love—"

When Gemma sank to her knees, I tried to hold her up, but she ignored me. Shit, if she wrapped that heaven-sent mouth of hers over me, I was a goner. *Done.* I'd be coming in seconds. But as she pumped me, I cared less and less about prolonging this and more and more about coming.

She shifted her body and mine, pressing me back against the wall. Thank God, because I needed the support. Was it possible to die from pleasure? I was willing to find out. Her warm breath on the crown of my cock had me vibrating, and I clawed at the wall for support. When she wrapped her lips around me, I groaned in surrender and dug my hands into her hair. Gemma lapped the length of me before circling the tip in a deliberate motion. When she teased my piercing with the tip of her tongue, I begged. I wasn't proud of it, but there it was.

Hands in her hair, head leaning back against the wall, eyes squeezed shut, praying not to come, I ground out, "Jesus, love. Gems, I can't bloody..." Fuck it, I couldn't think and words were.... Fuck, I had no words.

Her skilled hands wrapped around my girth as she stroked in time with her suckling mouth, and blood roared through my head. I clamped a fist in my mouth in an attempt to steady myself against my release. But it didn't do any good. A wave of pleasure crashed into me, making my legs shake, and nearly felled me as I came.

Holy... Shit...

Gemma grinned up at me. "I have been dying to do that."

I couldn't speak. For several moments, I couldn't move but managed to mumble, "You can do that anytime you want. No arguments from me."

She stood and turned from me, but I dragged her back. "Where do you think you're going? I'm not done with you."

"I certainly hope not. I have plans for you."

"Oh yeah? I'm all yours." I kissed her neck. On wobbly legs, I led us slowly to the bed. Any faster and my knees would have given out. I placed her on the bed, crawling in behind her. When I inhaled deeply, my dick twitched. Bugger. How could I possibly be ready again? I was pretty sure I was ready to pass out.

Gemma turned in the circle of my arms and kissed my pectoral gently. A smile tugged at her lips when I groaned and tightened my hands on her ass. "I can feel that, you know."

I chuckled against her neck. "I can't help it. You smell bloody incredible. So really this is your fault." As I ran a hand through her hair, I tugged the strands gently. "I can't seem to stop."

"I don't want you to stop." Using her teeth, she grazed my nipple gently, and I hissed.

"Naughty little minx." Before she could protest, I

rolled us over and had her pinned beneath me. My piercing slid over her wet heat,. the smooth tip of me swelling at the delicious friction, more than ready and willing to go... again.

"Matthias." She laughed. "What kind of vitamins are you on? Honestly, I could use them to keep me alert during stakeouts."

I nuzzled her neck, and my chest vibrated as I laughed. "Not vitamins, love. You, Gemma. You're guaranteed to keep me ready and willing all night." I nipped at the skin in the hollow just under her ear. "And all morning." With my tongue, I licked down the column of her throat. "And all afternoon. Through afternoon tea. Pretty much, if a man is around you, he's going to be hard. I know I am. Just thinking about you is enough to do it."

She rolled her eyes. "Oh, really? Just what part of me is inducing such enthusiasm? Is it the breasts?"

I chuckled low, as my gaze dipped. "Well, they do have a way of distracting me."

She bit back a moan as I circumvented her breasts and kissed down her belly. "Okay, Matthias, then tell me. Is it my ass?"

I paused my kisses just over her sex, and she arched into me, lifting her hips toward my mouth. I took the opportunity to palm both of her cheeks and squeeze.

Fuck, I loved her curves. It made me think about some of the things I'd seen at the club Rafe had taken me to. Some of the things I wanted to try with her.

"Okay, I'm not going to lie. That has a little to do with it." I used my grip to hold her in place as I placed my lips over her clit and sucked.

Gemma screamed. The sharp pull of need had her rolling toward the edge of orgasm quickly. But I was determined not to rush. With my thumbs, I parted her soft folds. With long laps of my tongue, I thoroughly loved her, alternating between licking her folds, sucking on her clit, and teasing soft circles over it with my tongue. Gemma gasped when I ran my tongue down to the tight stretch of skin between her slick center and her ass. I'd taken my lessons at the club very seriously. But I watched and paid attention to what seemed to make her hotter.

When I slid two fingers into her, she bucked. But it wasn't until I replaced my fingers with my tongue that she clamped her legs down around me.

With a grunt, I wedged her legs apart with my broad shoulders. I used my hands to hold her in place as I fucked her with my tongue, working it in and out of her. She clutched at the pillows behind her wildly, unable to breathe as I shoved her toward orgasm.

"Matthias, please... "

Her breath caught, and I replaced my tongue with two fingers, curling them, and rubbing lightly over her G-spot.

She groaned. "Oh. My. God. Jesus." Lacing her hands in the thick strands of my hair, she tugged in an attempt to drag me up her body, but I just chuckled.

"Sweetheart, relax. I'll get there, I promise. Right now, I want to play a little."

And play I did. With two fingers sliding into her slick channel and my tongue on her clit, I licked and teased her, drawing out the pleasure. But I wasn't satisfied until she was heading toward the cliff again. I rotated my hand as I teased her clit with my teeth, ever so slightly. I lit her body on fire when I applied a little pressure with my teeth and simultaneously grazed her tight rosette with my thumb. Her body started to quake.

Gently circling my thumb, I whispered, "Your body is incredible, Gemma. All the things I've missed out on, I want to experience with you. Anything you want, I'll give it to you."

"Matthias, please. I'm begging you. I need you. Please just—"

"I want it all with you, Gemma. I want to give you everything" I released her, despite her moans and kissed my way back up her body.

I lined my cock up to her heat. "Is this okay? I can get a condom. I just—I want to feel you."

"Yes, I'm on the pill. Please. I need you inside me. I can't wait."

When I slid my cock deep into her, she was more than ready. Our bodies melted together like they belonged. Like one would die without the other.

My eyes nearly crossed as the heat trapped me in. We knew this wasn't about sex. We were making love. She held on tight to me as I stroked deep inside her, then retreated until I was almost fully out, then drove back home again.

She felt so damn good. So perfect, like she was made for me. I kissed her softly and cupped her face as I made love to her. "Gemma, I don't ever want to leave."

Her inner walls fluttered, beginning to milk me, and I dropped my forehead to hers. "Stay with me, love. You are everything I didn't know I deserved. I love you so much."

Gemma reached up and cupped my face. And I knew the truth before she spoke the words. "I've always loved you."

With those words, I couldn't hold on to the reigns of control any longer. Hands fisting in her hair, I let instinct take over as I claimed her. Kissing her and growling low, I insisted she come. With a series of shallow strokes, I kept up a teasing pace until she threw her head back and screamed my name.

With her pulsing around me, I let go of my control. Nipping at her neck, I roared and broke apart in her arms. The orgasm rolled through her and rendered my brain officially useless. With a shudder over her, I groaned and collapsed.

10

———

Matthias

I RAN my hands over my face again. I was so fucking in love with Gemma, it was terrifying, but also amazing. She was mine.

Yeah, enjoy the warm fuzzy mate, just hurry the fuck up and check out. You've already dawdled too long. Making love to her had taken time we probably didn't have, but I didn't give a fuck.

Despite everything going on, I grinned. The feeling was almost foreign, like my cheeks wanted to rebel against the strange sensation of my skin stretching ear to ear. It was stupid, but I was just plain... happy. Even with killers plotting against me I still had something I'd never had before.

Gemma.

I pulled the door to the motel office open and a bell jingled, but no one was at the front desk. We needed to get our shit and go. We'd already stayed longer than I'd intended. Where was everyone?

I couldn't deny that I was happy to have some time alone with Gemma before we were stuck in the penthouse with everyone else. They were my family, but all the guys who worked for Blake Security were nosy as hell. I doubted we'd have much privacy with each of them asking all the probing questions and trying their damnedest to embarrass me. Not that I could blame them. If one of the other guys suddenly showed up with a long-lost girlfriend, I'd be giving them shit too. And I'd also be a skeptical motherfucker. There would be some raised eyebrows for certain, given how much Oskar liked to gossip. They probably all knew the sordid details.

But soon they'd get it. It didn't take long around Gemma to feel how genuine she was. It radiated off her like sunlight. Something that hadn't changed since she was a kid. It had always made me feel like I was willing to do anything for her just to see her smile. The thought made me move faster. I wanted to see that smile again.

And I'd find all the ways to make her smile as soon as we were safe.

I rang the bell that apparently woke the clerk. He came out from the back, with his clothes rumpled and drool still in his scruffy salt and pepper beard. "Can I help you?"

"Yeah, checking out of room twelve."

He frowned. "You Australian or something like that? Don't remember no Australian."

My stare must have communicated that I didn't want to shoot the breeze or engage in any small talk because he turned to the computer and started typing. He walked over to the ancient printer in the corner and waited as the machine. The first sheet came out crumpled and ripped. After a few muffled curses, he came back to the computer and started typing again.

I could practically feel my blood pressure rising. What the hell could be taking so long? This place was a dump so I doubted Gemma had paid much of a security deposit or would have any charges against her account. It wasn't like this place had room service.

When the printer spit out another crumpled sheet, I groaned.

"Look, mate. I'm kind of in a hurry. Can I just leave the key in the room when we go? I don't even care about the deposit. We'll be gone in five minutes."

His eyes lit up at that. "Of course. Have a good day."

My lips twisted at that. Now he wanted to be polite? I jogged back to the room, ready to grab Gemma and get the hell out of here.

"All right, luv. Time to go." I paused when I crossed the threshold, my eyes taking in the state of the room.

The covers and sheets on the bed were tossed to the floor. The chair in front of the desk was overturned and Gemma's bag was in the middle of the floor instead of by the bed where I'd left it. My stomach dropped as it registered that the room was empty.

"Gemma!" I raced through the room, sticking my head into the bathroom to make sure she wasn't there. Nothing. My pulse was a drumbeat as I ran back to the front door and burst out into the afternoon sunlight. My eyes scanned the perimeter of the lot, searching for movement. Anything.

The parking lot was empty.

Cursing, I ran back into the room. I snatched my phone out of the pocket of my jeans and dialed Rafe. "Gemma's gone," I barked as soon as the other man answered.

"What do you mean gone? She left?"

"No, she was taken."

"Did you see the assailant?"

I could hear the sudden rush of Rafe's breathing. He

was running, probably to the garage. The mental image was something for me to hold on to, and so I did, concentrating on it hard. Anything to avoid thinking about Gemma scared and possibly hurt.

"No. I was checking out. When I came back she was already gone."

"I hate to be the one to ask, kid. But are you sure she didn't leave on her own?"

I gripped the phone tightly. My eyes swung over to the bed, to the thing I hadn't been able to handle looking at.

"There's blood on the sheets, Rafe."

After a brief pause, I heard the other man cursing.

"Get back to headquarters. I'll brief the others." Then the line went dead.

Over the next few minutes, I had to credit my training as the only reason I managed to stay upright. Methodically, I checked the room to be sure there was nothing left behind that might provide a clue as to who had taken Gemma. We'd come back here to get her stuff, but her bag was still here. Another reason I knew she hadn't gone willingly. Why would she disappear without her supplies and money?

On the drive back to the penthouse, I mentally reviewed all the possible suspects. Of course, Gemma was ORUS, so there were any number of people who'd have a grudge but for them to take her quickly and efficiently meant they were highly trained. This wasn't just some random person with an axe to grind.

The thought of that didn't make me feel better. It would have been easier if this were some misguided asshole on a revenge quest. They'd likely have underestimated Gemma and she'd have had them flat on their ass before they could even get her ten feet. But no, they'd managed to take her with no trace at all, so it was definitely someone highly trained.

They'd also gone in while I wasn't there, which meant they had eyes and ears in the room and had likely been following us all day. Otherwise, how would they have been able to strike at precisely the right time? It was a hard pill to swallow to think someone had been following us and able to evade notice, but I had to admit that my concentration was compromised around Gemma. It was entirely possible that someone had been following us and I'd missed the signs. Something that was hard on the ego but necessary to admit if we were going to find her.

As soon as I entered the penthouse, Rafe started talking.

"Noah is on the phone with Ian now. This isn't ORUS. Oskar is digging deeper on the Family to find out if any of their operatives are in town. We're going to find her, kid."

My breath felt like it was stuck in my throat. Up until that very moment, I'd kept my thoughts on the task of getting her back. I'd kept my brain methodical and logical because going anywhere else was too much. Thinking of where she was right now, whether she was scared or hurt, was too much. But when Rafe said it out loud, it made it real somehow.

Gemma was gone.

"Fuck, man. They must have taken her as soon as I left the room. I was right there. I let her down."

"This isn't the time to blame yourself, kid. Hell, you can do that later if you want, but that shit isn't going to get us closer to finding your girl. We need you sharp. Because those fuckers aren't going to get away with this. You have all of Blake Security behind you."

While we were talking Oskar, Noah, and Ryan had come into the room. Oskar and Jonas hung back a little, but Noah walked over and after a brief hesitation, put a heavy hand on my head. It was an odd gesture, almost paternal, and though part of me wanted to flinch at the connection, there was a deeper part that craved it, too. For so many years, I was on my own and had no one to trust or rely on. But this was too much for me to tackle alone. And I was beyond grateful that the others had my back.

"I know this is a lot to ask, especially considering all that's happened. But I need to get her back. She's my... She's just mine." I stammered, not sure exactly what I was trying to say but Noah just smiled.

"We know, kid. That's why we're going to come up with a plan. None of us will rest until you have her back. She's family now. And no one fucks with our family."

———

Gemma

IT WAS DARK. And so cold.

I shivered, wondering what happened to my blanket. My thoughts were slow and thick, like they were running through molasses. Then I remembered that we were at the hotel. Matthias should have come out of the shower by now.

I tried to sit up, stopped by a sharp tug at my wrists. Panic clawed at the edges of my thoughts, but the emotional response was muted and seemed faraway.

Everything seemed almost like it was happening to someone else.

Drugged. You've been drugged.

My training had taught me the importance of staying calm, so I stopped moving and took several deep breaths. It was likely that whatever drug they'd given me was wearing off and if I stayed still and quiet, perhaps I could gain enough strength to fight when my captors returned.

Even though I still couldn't move well, my thoughts and memories were starting to come back. Bits and pieces from earlier in the day started to return. After flying back from Canada, we'd gone straight to the motel to get my stuff. I could remember that clearly. Matthias had been happy, smiling—something I was pretty sure was rare.

He loves me.

The thought made me smile. It was something I doubted he'd ever told another woman. Just the thought of other women around Matthias made the green-eyed monster roar in anger. I'd never been the jealous type before but with him, it was different. He was mine and a part of me felt that he'd always been mine.

But after the images of us together at the motel, things started to get fuzzy. Hazy images of lovemaking floated through my head; I could definitely remember us going at it hard. But after that, nothing. How could I just go to sleep and then not remember a damn thing?

For me to be in this position, someone had to have broken into the room, and I apparently slept through the whole thing.? My head pounded. None of this made any sense. The only way I would sleep through a break-in was if I'd been drugged beforehand.

Was that it? Had someone managed to slip me something before we even reached the motel?

Just then, the sound of a door opening jarred me from my thoughts. I attempted to look completely still and peaceful, hoping whoever it was would think I was still asleep.

"It's no use pretending. I know you're awake."

The deep voice was immediately recognizable. Father.

Oh shit.

If he's here, then that means I'm...

"Where am I?"

He chuckled lightly. "Back at home where you belong. Clearly I was asking too much of you with this mission."

My heart sank. If I was back with the Family, then there was no way Matthias could find me. He wouldn't be looking for me in London. And the Family had all the resources necessary to fly a body across the pond without anyone asking questions.

"So you drugged me and then put me on a plane?"

It was then that I discovered the room wasn't dark. I'd just been too weak to open my eyes until now. But as I looked around, I could tell that I was tethered to an iron ring in the floor. There was a curtain preventing me from seeing the rest of the room.

I must be at the compound. Otherwise they wouldn't care if I saw the room.

They'd inadvertently given something away here, and I didn't think they even realized it. I smiled.

"How long have I been asleep?"

"Too long. Sabine was starting to get worried about you." His voice was amused, as if he enjoyed allowing my friend to worry that I might not wake up.

Sadistic bastard.

"I was making progress. If you'd only given me more time—"

"Enough!"

His sudden shout ricocheted through the room, and I flinched away at the sound. My wrists were bound tightly together behind me, but instinct had me trying to raise them anyway, ready to ward off any blows. Every ORUS agent was trained for moments like this. No one could execute these types of missions without contemplating the reality of death.

I'd thought about this so many times and always thought I'd be more afraid. But I wasn't really afraid for myself. My thoughts were for all the other people I'd let down. My mother. Sabine.

Matthias.

They were all going to suffer if I didn't find a way out of this. My mother would wonder if my training had been lacking. She'd beat herself up thinking that she hadn't done enough to prepare me.

Sabine would give up; I knew it. She'd always been soft-hearted, and the reality of this life had broken her in some ways. Without the hope of me coming for her, she'd lose the last bit of innocence that was keeping her the same little girl I used to play with. She'd be just like the other women here with soft voices and vacant expressions, empty inside and resigned to their fate. Just the thought of it broke me.

Then there was Matthias. My sweet Matt who'd grown up to be the fierce warrior that I always knew he would be. He'd gone from cold and closed-off to tentatively starting to trust again.

What was he thinking about my disappearance? Did he think I'd abandoned him? That thought hurt more than any other, and I curled into myself. Did he think I'd run and left him? Would he even look for me? Why had no one ever prepared me for this type of wound?

"He's going to come for me. You know that." I told the lie as if it were truth. My voice betrayed none of the pain inside. I could pride myself on that.

There was a rustling sound, like fabric sliding against fabric. Was he sitting down? From behind the curtain, I had no sense of the room where I was being held. But if I could hear him moving around, maybe I could get a sense of the layout.

"Yes. He will come for you. That is the whole point of this little exercise. You don't honestly think I would have gone to all this trouble for just you?"

There was a quiet satisfaction in his voice that terrified me.

He was right. Everything I knew about Matthias said he'd come for me. And he'd be walking into a trap.

"That's what you were counting on," I whispered. I felt like an idiot for not considering it before. Father was all about the endgame. His goal was to get to Matthias. If he couldn't get to him in New York, then the next-best option was to force him to come back to where it all began.

"I wasn't on a mission, was I?"

He didn't speak for a moment, and I wondered if that was how he planned to torment me. Leave me here alone with my questions and my regret. But then he answered.

"No, you were on a mission. It just wasn't the mission you thought it was."

There was more rustling, and since my ears were trained to it now, I could tell that he was standing up, probably straightening his suit. King of all he surveyed. This was just another day to him. Business as usual.

"In two days' time, this will all be over. Then I can finally finish this the way it should have been done years ago. You won't rise from the dead a second time."

A door closed, and I was alone again.

And all I could do was wait and pray. Pray that Matthias didn't come for me.

11

———

Matthias

A GRENADE. I needed a damn grenade. I was tired of waiting. I knew Noah said we needed to plan first, but every moment that ticked by was a moment she needed me.

My guns were ready. My vest and back holster were loaded down. I also had another piece strapped to my ankle. And then there were the knives. Those were a given. My favorites were the ones Noah had custom made for me. They were designed to slot into my vest undetected, but as this was a special occasion, I wanted more. So much more.

Those fuckers had taken Gemma. *My* Gemma. Did they really think I wouldn't come for them? If so, they were seriously mistaken, because now it was time to blow some shit up.

More like shoot them in a noncritical part of their bodies, then have a little fun with knives, and then burn everything to the ground. I didn't know what would happen next. I knew I wasn't supposed to let that part of myself out. It was the programming. But I didn't care, because for once, that monster was going to be good for something.

My mobile rang, and I answered on the first ring. "What?"

"I have the information you asked for."

Dane.

Dane was the closest thing I'd had to a friend at ORUS before Noah. We hadn't been super close, but we'd both come from the Family. Dane had been handed off to ORUS a couple of years before I had.

Back in the Family, we'd known each other peripherally. Dane had mostly kept to himself. He'd been a scrawny kid. Quiet. He'd mostly stayed under the radar. I wondered what the hell he'd had to do to get himself handed over to ORUS.

Once at ORUS, we'd just been agents. Neither one of

us could ever talk about what had happened, how we had gotten there, or who we were before.

But it had been Dane who had noticed what I'd been up to. He'd warned me, told me that going after the Family would have some dire consequences.

That's where we were different. While Dane had been mostly surviving—being an agent, doing his job, and keeping his head down—I couldn't live like that. I had to make things right.

Over the course of a year, Dane had kept me abreast of the Family's movements until the last time we'd seen each other when he'd point-blank told me that the Family was coming for me. But had I listened? No. Like a bloody wanker, I'd thought I was untouchable. And now Gemma was paying for that mistake.

I'd texted Dane with an SOS as soon as Gemma was gone, hoping that the old ties would at least give me some direction.

"I found someone for you. He's Family. He moved to New York three years ago. It looks like he's been loaned out to the De Santos family, mostly drug running. He's an intermediary, pretty much. I'll text you his address."

"Thank you. Listen, when this is over, you don't owe me anything anymore. You should, you know, get on with your life and shit. If I were you, I'd get out of ORUS."

There was a moment of silence. When Dane spoke, his voice was low but flat. "Not all of us are you, Matthias. Even when we were kids, you saw what was going on, and you opted to do something about it. That was never me. Maybe it's time I learn to do more than just survive."

I clamped my jaw to stamp out the well of emotion. When I spoke, it was through clenched teeth. "Yeah, mate. Thanks."

"If you need any help going in to get her, you know where to find me."

"Yeah, mate. I do." I hung up and finished with the weapons. I had enough ammo to last one long-ass gunfight. And if and when I was out of weapons, I would let out the monster and kill them all. That sounded like a good plan to me. When I turned around, I stopped short. "Fuck, mate. What the fuck?"

Delaney was leaning in the doorway to the weapons room. "Are you going somewhere?"

"Get out of my way. I need to go get Gemma."

Delaney crossed his arms, looking not at all like he was trying to move. The kid should really know better. It was funny that I referred to Delaney as the kid, because I was pretty sure Delaney was older than me. "No. You just got back. After everything that happened, don't you think you need your team right now?"

"No. Gemma's mine. Someone took her. I'm going to get her back."

"Forgive me if I'm wrong, but when crazy Rafe came to this penthouse, didn't we stand with Noah? When that fucking psychotic douche bag came after JJ and took the baby, didn't we stand as a house? When Diana's brothers tried to end her, didn't we all fight together? What makes you any different?"

What the hell was that burning sensation in the center of my chest? *It's called emotions, asshole.* "That was different. I'm just going to get information right now."

"No, you're not."

I hated to do this. I really did. I'd always liked Delaney. But the kid was standing in the way, between me and Gemma. When I sauntered over to Delaney, the guy didn't even flinch, which, honestly, I had to give him credit for. After all, I was armed to the teeth, and for the most part, a homicidal maniac. At least I felt that way right now.

"I don't want to hurt you, so just pass on by. Let me go."

"No. I'm not going to do that. We're family, so where you go, *we* go."

I didn't really have time for this shit. "How about if I told you I was just running to the store for some milk, would you believe me?" Delaney just narrowed his eyes.

"Listen. That was a friend of mine on the phone. He sent me a contact, and the bloke will get squirrely if I don't show. I'm not letting any of you lot get in the way of my one chance to get information about Gemma. Do I make myself clear?"

Delaney seemed to ponder this, and then he stepped aside. "This is a mistake. Y Going in blind, without backup, that's going to get you *and* her killed."

"Haven't you heard? I'm the Shadow. I'm impossible to kill."

I turned with my weapons in hand and headed for the door. I only hoped I was right.

Gemma

"Oh, bloody hell."

For the first time in a long time, I let myself slip into my natural accent. I'd been feigning being an American for so long that it had become the dominant one. But in times of stress, I became just another East End guttersnipe.

The damn ropes were tight. At some point a couple

of hours ago, somebody had come in and moved me to a chair. I didn't know why they hadn't used zip ties. I at least knew how to break out of those. This rope shit was impossible. I couldn't see what they'd done and without a visual, it would be nearly impossible to slip whatever knot they'd used.

I was more alert now. Unfortunately, that meant my mind was going a mile a minute. Going over every mistake, every piece of the plan I'd overlooked. Where had things gone wrong? The more I played it in my mind, the less sense it made. We'd been so careful. *I* had been so careful.

After returning from Toronto, we'd gone straight to the penthouse. Matthias and I had only gone back to the motel to get my things. It was so stupid. After all, they were only things. Why did I even leave the safety of the penthouse? Oh God, had they hurt Matthias? My whole plan was fucked. I was supposed to be out there helping civilians, saving the world, getting Father. I was supposed to walk away from this. But instead, I'd ended up right back where I'd started. And this time, there was no Matthias to look out for me, no one to protect me, no one but myself. *You better figure that shit out.*

Again, I tried the knot, more gently this time. I tried to determine the gauge and feel of it. This wasn't like a pair of cuffs where I could simply break my thumb easily. These were bound tight on my wrist, giving no opportunity for movement. The way they chafed, I was pretty sure I'd have scars moving forward.

Yeah, if I lived that long... and because there was no way out, my brain kept playing the game of *how did you end up here*? My best guess was they'd had someone watching the penthouse. Sure, Matthias had taken hyper-evasive movements, but Father could have had someone watching me from the moment I arrived in New York, so they might have discovered the hotel I'd stayed in. It wasn't the one they'd insisted I use. Truth be told, I didn't make any mistake. But once again, my actions had put Matthias at risk.

Please, God, let him be okay.

The door creaked open, and I held still. I couldn't talk as they'd gagged me when they moved me to the chair. So all I could do was pray.

"What the hell are you doing back here?"

That voice, it shouldn't have filled me with a sense of relief, but it did. Shame, as well. Worry. And Sadness. Sabine had come to find me. The friend I was supposed to be saving was now on a mission to save me.

"You shouldn't have come back for me."

I craned my head as Sabine took out my gag. "I wasn't supposed to leave you here this long. I'm so sorry."

"Don't be sorry." My friend shook her dark locks. "I didn't want you to come back to this. No. I wouldn't want this for anyone."

"You are my friend, and I gave you my word. I told you I was going to come for you, and I did. It's just not exactly the way I had planned."

"You really shouldn't have come back. I don't know what this is going to mean for you."

I narrowed my gaze on Sabine as she brushed her hair behind her ear. She had a dark bruise along her jaw. "Did someone hurt you?"

Sabine immediately flicked her hair so it covered her face. "It's fine. We need to get you out of here. Let me see if I can do something about the ropes."

While she was examining the ropes around my wrists, I mentally reviewed several exit strategies. "If we work together, we can get out of here. I just need to know how many guards are at the exits. The laundry room—the one with the tunnel—is that still open?"

It was a wild hope. I didn't even know for sure where I was. I assumed that they'd taken me back to the warehouse in the UK, but there was no telling how long I'd been out. I could have been out an hour, and we might be in upstate New York. Hell, we could be down the street from Matthias right now, and he wouldn't know. I wouldn't know.

"Sabine, do you know where we are? Do you know—"

Sabine shook her head. "No, please don't ask me that. Otherwise, they'll make this look like a walk in the park." She indicated the side of her face as she turned her head away and then went back to working on the ropes. It took several moments, but finally they loosened a little bit.

"There. You should be able to get one hand out and put it back. I pretty much worked at the same knot and just made a looser version of it. You should be able to get your hand in and out of this now."

I pulled one hand out, wincing as the rope abraded my skin. "*Jesus Christ.*" My hand was raw and red. It was bleeding in a couple of spots where the skin had been scraped off. I might be able to reduce the burning sting if I had a first aid kit, but it was unlikely they had any of those here. "Listen to me. I know you're scared, but I can protect you. There are people coming. All right? Help is on the way."

"There's no help on the way. No one is coming for me."

"Sabine, look at me. I have someone who loves me. With me gone, he's going to raise hell until he finds me. And he's lethal. He will come for us. That's what Father wanted all along. And when he comes, you're leaving with us." I didn't tell her that it was Matt from our childhood. The less she knew, the less she could inadvertently reveal.

Sabine narrowed her gaze and then brought out her bottle of water. "Drink this. Your man, he sounds almost as dangerous as this lot." Her South London accent reminded me so much of my childhood. It reminded me so much of the horrors I'd left behind but of the good memories, as well.

"He is more dangerous than they are. But he's also one of the good guys. And he's not leaving me here."

Sabine nodded her head. "I'm glad for you then. But when he comes for you, I'm expendable. You're the one he wants."

"Listen to me. He's coming for me, but he'll take you because I won't leave without you. So he really won't have a choice. But, like I said, he's one of the good guys. He wouldn't consciously leave here with them. Not with them. He hates them almost as much as we do."

"You talk about him like he's the second coming."

"No, he's not quite an angel. He's more like the shadow that stalks angels. But he's mine. And he's coming for us. You just wait. In the meantime, we need to figure our own way out. Because when he comes, they're not just going to let him take us. They want him dead. They want to destroy everything he's about. They want him to suffer. So, it's going to require us to fight. And we need to be ready."

Sabine nodded. "Okay. Whatever you say. I'll be ready to go. And I... Thank you for everything. I don't think I've ever had a friend quite like you before."

"Don't thank me yet. You thank me when we're sitting in my flat back in New York, okay? That's when you thank me. But for now, lay low. Get ready to fight, because he's coming and he's bringing a lot of help with him."

12

———

Matthias

THE THING WAS people were rarely ready for the unexpected. Oftentimes people wanted to profess that they were ready and they knew what was coming for them, but I thrived on the unexpected. I lived in those unexpected shadows.

As I tucked my phone back into my jacket pocket, I silently applied the decryption for the keypad lock and let it do its thing. In seconds, it was green.

I'd already bypassed the security system. In seconds, as soundlessly as a movie ninja, I was inside the house. Ryder, Dane's contact, apparently thought that mere locks with government encryptions would keep some-body out.

The problem was it seemed no one told Ryder just how good I was at hacking. When I found him, he was sitting in front of the television, with his back to the hall.

Another rookie mistake. Never have your back to the exits. In seconds, I had my arm around Ryder's neck in a modified arm bar, and boy did he flop around like a fish. The wild thrashing only lasted for a hair of a second though, and then Ryder was trying to employ all his defensive skills to get himself turned around. But I just pressured the trachea and then leaned forward. "There, there, calm down. It's just me. First, you're going to go to sleep. And then you and I are going to have a little chat, because I'm not willing to take no for an answer."

More thrashing came about. As it was, Ryder didn't seem to know what was good for him. Eventually, I could see the signs of him fading, the fight slowly leaking out of him like a slow drip. Then finally, he stopped moving.

For a long second, I wondered if I'd killed him. *Good on ya, mate.*

But a quick check of the pulse told me I hadn't. It only took two minutes to get the zip ties and a chair and have Ryder positioned. Honestly, the hardest part of the break-in was moving Ryder's dead weight into the chair.

But once I had him positioned, I used a smelling salt to wake the little wanker.

Ryder choked and coughed and immediately tried to thrash his limbs around. "What the fuck, you psychopath? Father will end you."

I grinned. "So you've heard of me. Brilliant. And, actually, it turns out I'm not a psychopath. A doctor told me that, so it must be true, eh? Apparently, you lot in the Family did something to me. I'm not a psychopathic killer at all, which is a relief. I was really starting to worry about that. But, that doesn't mean I'm not dangerous."

I leaned nice and close to Ryder's face as I played with one of my knives. I flicked my fingertip over the very tippy top and then mulled over the drop of red that appeared on my fingertip. When I sucked it into my mouth, the brassy taste assaulted my tongue. But I lifted my gaze to my quarry and made it a point to look like I was enjoying myself.

"Now, why don't you go ahead and tell me what I need to know, or it'll be your blood on the tip of this knife. What do you say?"

"Fuck you."

"You know, it's weird because that saying has a lot more meaning to me now, mate. But that's neither here nor there. What is here and there is that you're going to give me the information I need. I'm very, very good, but I'm fresh out of fucks and patience at the moment. And I don't want to fuck up and kill you because I'm one of the good guys now. Tell me what I need to know, and you'll wake up tomorrow, a little bit groggy and not missing any limbs. How does that sound?"

Ryder's eyes went wide as if judging if I would dismember him. The reputation I'd built over the years was serving me well. But there was a small part of me that didn't want to have people look at me like that.

You are not this person. You're just doing the job you need to do.

"So, what do you say? Are we going to do this the easy way? Because I don't have a lot of time and I need to get to Gemma. I need to get to her now."

Ryder's eyes went wide, and he struggled against his restraints.

"Get to talking. I don't have a lot of time, and I'm not feeling real patient." I did the knife thing again and he shuddered.

"Okay... I'll tell you what you want to know."

"Cheers, mate. No one needs to bleed today... too badly anyway."

———

Matthias

DEEP BREATH IN. Count to three. Deep breath out. Deep breath in. Count to three. Deep breath out. I repeated this to myself over and over again as I left. I felt a little out of my body, like something was off, something was missing... like I'd forgotten something.

A part of me waited for the monster to stretch, to demand to be let out, to demand to go back and finish the job. But no, there was none of that. Instead, there was something slightly empty. It was as if the monster that had been attached to my back for the last several years was no longer there.

Not that I wasn't still an efficient killer. A deadly one, if I chose to be. But now, I felt as if I was the one in control instead of being merely the one in charge of keeping the monster under control. I'd left Ryder alive. The fucker was still strapped to his chair.

But he was a member of the Family. He'd figure out how to get out eventually when he woke up out of his stupor. By then, I would be long gone and hopefully have Gemma back. And I sure as hell wasn't worried about any repercussions. Ryder was of *them*. He'd gotten off lucky.

I rounded the corner and stopped short. "Fuck a twat."

"Easy there, Prince Charming. Would you use language like that during afternoon tea?"

I glared at Oskar. The big German stood against the lamppost, legs crossed, arms folded over his massive chest, looking at ease and completely comfortable. Rafe was with him and leaned comfortably on the hood of my Tesla. Fucking ruining the bloody shine.

Oskar just shook his head. "You don't look happy to see us. Rafe, buddy, it doesn't look like he's happy to see us."

Rafe tsked. "No, it does not. Do you want to tell us why you're not happy to see us, kid?" Rafe pushed himself up off the car, making it a point to get finger-prints all over it. I wasn't picky about anything. Hell, I barely owned anything. The one material thing I cared about though was that car. And now Rafe had his bloomin' mitts all over it.

"Mate, get your grubby mitts off my car."

Rafe just shrugged. "Make me."

I glared at him. "I don't have fucking time for this. I don't have time for your scolding and your antics." I took several steps toward Rafe, and Oskar stepped in my path.

"Easy does it, kid. We have some questions for you."

Oskar put a hand on my chest, and I glared down at it. "Are you a nutter, mate?"

A week ago, none of the lads, even Noah, would have put a hand on me like this. Touching was always an iffy spot with me.

"Yeah, maybe a little. You left without your team."

"Listen, I don't have time to hold your fucking wanker for you. I had to get moving. I had intel from a contact to get. There was no time."

Rafe finally stopped manhandling my car and walked around. I was still completely at ease, sensing no aggression coming off of him. "Oh yeah, Delaney was strapping-up to the teeth to come get you when we got home and he told us you'd booked without so much as a by-your-leave. There wasn't time to tell us then?"

I rolled my shoulders. "You would have stopped me."

"Oskar, tell your friend what he clearly seems to have forgotten: we are family. That means when one person in this family has a problem, we *all* have a problem. Therefore, we take backup."

I rolled my eyes. "Do I look like I fuckin' need backup, mate?" I gestured back toward the house. "I obviously had it handled. I got the information I needed, and I didn't need you for that. Besides, after everything, I just—"

Both Oskar and Rafe grabbed their weapons and,

without blinking an eye, raised them in my direction and fired.

In that fine line between knowledge and the subconscious, I gleaned the danger and hit the deck. I was only able to get one gun out.

I'd be able to take one of them out if needed, but the other was going to definitely shoot me. What the fuck?

It was only after I palmed my weapon that my brain triggered and started using all the synapses it had. I hadn't been hit. They hadn't fired at me. Rafe was a crack shot. Oskar might even be a better shot than Rafe, and that was saying something. So why wasn't I hit?

Slowly, I rolled onto my back and aimed my gun in the same direction as they fired again.

Ryder was on the ground. "Jesus fucking Christ!"

I lay back on the hard concrete, my breath jaggedly tearing in and out of my lungs.

Oskar leaned over me in a squatting stance, hands placed on his knees. "You see, kid, that's why you bring back up, because sometimes, motherfuckers are slick. And they think they can get the jump on you."

I blinked rapidly. Ryder had gotten loose? But how? Maybe he hadn't been knocked out after all.

Shit. Careless.

Somewhere in the far recesses of my mind, a last smidgeon of my monster tried to shout out, '*You should have just killed him.*' But I was able to shut that thought down easily enough.

When I slid a glance over at Rafe, he just shrugged and re-holstered his weapon. "You can relax. He's not dead." Rafe reached down a palm for one of my hands and Oskar did the same for the other.

For a long second, I stared at their outreached hands, symbols of olive branches. Maybe I wasn't supposed to do this alone. Maybe I could actually lean on family for once. I re-holstered my weapon, then took both their hands, and was up in a second.

"I have an address for the Family's transporter here in New York. He'll be able to tell us how they got her out and, at the very least, where they're taking her."

Oskar nodded. "Yep, sounds good. But first, here you go."

He handed me the comm unit and I stuck it in my ear, adjusting it so it fit. "What channel are we on?"

Rafe automatically mumbled, "Three."

I tapped the unit three times and said, "Mic check."

Oskar said, "Clear."

Rafe echoed the sentiment. And then there was another voice in my ear. "I hear you loud and clear."

I held my breath. "Noah?"

"Hey, kid. I hear you went out on a little excursion and hogged all the fun for yourself."

"Look, Noah, it's not what you think."

"So you mean you didn't leave me at home all by my lonesome to watch Rafe and Oskar brood about getting left behind?"

"Well, yeah. Okay, I did do that. But I had a reason."

"You're one of us now. Your past is our past. Your battles are ours too."

Oskar groaned. "Are we going to hug it out now, or should we go kill some assholes? Because someone promised me assholes, and I demand assholes."

Rafe chuckled. "Then you're easy to please. I have a mirror right here. Hold on."

Oskar just muttered under his breath, "Fucktard."

Rafe didn't miss a beat. "Don't be mad because I'm prettier than you are."

Oskar flashed a grin. "We all know I'm the prettiest one at the house. Matthias, tell him."

I slid my glance between the two of them and sighed. How was it that this ragtag bunch had become my family? At this point, I didn't really care. I was happy to have them, because without them, there was no way I was getting Gemma back. "I have the address. Who's ready for some assholes?"

Rafe and Oskar both raised their hands. Oskar added a little jump to his step. "Oh me, me. Please pick me. I want to kill the assholes first."

Noah just chuckled on the other end of the line. "Just punch in your coordinates when you get in the car and let me know if you need cleanup."

"Will do."

I climbed back in my car. It was time to go get my woman, by any means necessary.

———

Matthias

"Let me wake him up. I want to wake him up."

I rolled my eyes at Oskar. "I did the hard work of getting his name and location. I get to wake him up."

Rafe just shoved us aside. "I'm the most efficient. I should wake him up."

That was how Ryder's contact was woken out of a drug-induced stupor, with the three of us standing over him, wanting to deliver the first bout of ass kicking. Immediately he sat up and scooted back. "I don't have your drugs, man. I don't have anything you need. There's no money here."

I folded my arms and shook my head. "Now, now,

don't get your knickers in a twist. We're not here for money or drugs."

Maybe that wasn't the most reassuring thing I could have said, because the guy's eyes opened wide and he tried to shrink back even more against the headboard.

Oskar didn't help by leaning over the bed a little bit more. "You're what we're after."

There was never anything good about hearing a grown man whimper. And honestly, as ass-kickers went, Oskar was by far the least scary of the three of us. He was badass, but he hadn't gone through the kind of stuff that Rafe and I had gone through. At the core of Oskar there wasn't anything dark and scary. But the sniveling guy on the bed didn't know that. And given that Oskar, with his height, broad shoulders, and ice-blue eyes, resembled a Viking, it worked for intimidation tactics. But Oskar had no stomach for wet work. Come to think of it, I wasn't sure he'd ever killed anyone before.

In our little scenario, Rafe was acting as a good cop. "Relax. No one's going to kill you right now."

Oskar threw up his hands. "Why did you have to lie to the guy?"

Rafe just sighed. "It's called relaxing the subject. People are more likely to tell you things when they're calm. Not when you're peeling back their fingernails or threatening to cut off their balls. Honestly, don't you know this?"

While watching the three of us bicker was fun on most days, we didn't have time to waste. "If you lot are done, can we get back to the witness please? I need answers, and I need them now."

Rafe just rolled his eyes and nodded but grabbed the sniveling Aiden Wex by the shirt. "Come on powder puff. We have questions for you."

They guy wasn't small by any means. And it was a testament to Rafe's strength, the way he just held him up out of the bed like he weighed nothing. The guy was over two hundred pounds at least, but all of him soft. And what the hell? Was that the smell of... Oh hell, the guy had pissed himself.

For the love of Christ! "Mate, you're giving new meaning to taking the piss."

The German flashed me a grin, and I frowned. "What's so funny?"

Oskar shrugged. "Nothing, you just made a funny. I'm not used to it. It must be your shit-is-about-to-get-real demeanor."

I could only roll my eyes as we followed Rafe out to the living area where he'd already set up a chair with zip ties at the ready. "Is there any time when you're *not* joking around? You *look* so serious all the time that one would think that you'd actually be a serious person."

"I *am* a serious person. I just happen to have an amazing sense of humor. I can't believe you don't notice."

"Let's just fucking get to work, mate."

Rafe had the guy strapped in the chair in no time at all, almost like he'd done something like this before.

As much as we were joking around with each other, as soon as we had the guy where we wanted him, we went all business.

Rafe was the calmest. He had questions like: Where was the Family's facility? Where might they hide a prisoner? What were the transport routes?

Oskar was the menacing one. He just went on fully detailing all kinds of fascinating things about Viking conquest. Like what they liked to do with the skin and scalps of those they raided. And when it was my turn, I just sat in my chair across from the guy, took out my knives and started playing with them. And then very calmly I said, "You ran the shipping route for the Family. I would know, because I've been disrupting them for months. Last night, you had to sneak cargo out of here on one of your planes. I want to know exactly what route you took, where you landed, and the nearest

Family facilities surrounding that runway. Do you understand?"

And on and on it went like that for another forty-five minutes. All in all, it hadn't taken that long. But every minute it took with the three of us playing our roles to perfection was time Gemma didn't have.

At one point, Aiden started to cry. We hadn't even touched him at that point. It was then that I lost my temper. "I'm sick of playing these games. You're going to tell us what the fuck we want you to tell us now. Otherwise, I will kill you slowly. But I'll leave you tied up here first. When I finally find her, and if someone has even hurt so much as a hair on her head, I will come back for you. And I will draw out your killing and enjoy it. Do you understand me?"

A familiar flutter tickled at the back of my spine. One I was aware of and knew well, intimately. It was a feeling that had been missing over the last day and a half or so, despite tidbits of my monster trying to wake and take over again. I could feel the edges of my vision graying.

No. No. No. Not now.

We needed information. We didn't need this guy dead. I needed Gemma.

You are not a killer. It's not in your blood. You are in control.

The sound of the doctor's voice repeated over and over and over in my skull until the tingling stopped, cooled, and control was once again mine. But while I wrestled with control, I became more aware of my surroundings. Both Rafe and Oskar had their hands on their weapons. I tried to ignore the hurt of that. It was for their own safety. If I'd lost control again, they would have to put me down, as they should.

But I was in control again. Being in control meant I got to help save Gemma, which was all I wanted. "So why don't you tell us what we need to know?"

Aiden tried one last, gallant attempt at telling us to go and self-fornicate, but then I wrapped him in a head-lock and started to slowly squeeze the air from him. Just when Aiden's face went bright pink, I eased up on his trachea. Aiden dragged in several breaths and then I applied pressure again. One, two, three, release. Let him breathe. One, two, three. On and on it went for a good thirty seconds, and finally Aiden let go.

"Okay, okay. Just stop. Just stop. I was called and informed they had cargo and they needed to ship it overnight, immediately. I put them on a chartered flight. They left here at eleven last night and then arrived early in the morning in London. I would have said they'd taken it to main headquarters, but there is a smaller facility. West London actually. Chiswick. It's so posh out there that most people assume that the warehouses there are for shops. No one would ever think to look twice. If there was a facility good for hiding an unexpected shipment, that would be the one."

I leaned very close, my voice all ice and death. "See, was that so hard?" And then I proceeded to apply enough pressure to his trachea that Aiden went lights-out.

And as Aiden collapsed in my arms, I didn't even have an urge to kill him. We had what we wanted. Killing him wasn't even on the table anymore.

My, how far you've come.

13

─────────

Matthias

"Everybody knows the plan. Get in, get out, no unnecessary bodies. We're not supposed to be here."

Noah was on comms and I easily drowned him out. I loved Noah, but honestly, did he really think I was going to let these fuckers get away with taking Gemma? If anyone got in my way, they were going down. That was just the end of that.

On my left, I was flanked by Oskar, and on my right, by Rafe. We all had points of entry on the warehouse. On the other side, on the far corners, were Ryan and Dylan. Ian was on the east side with two of his men.

In and out, and we'd have her in no time. Planning was pretty basic. With the points of entry we had, we would converge in the center, find the best access points, get Gemma, and get out. Thanks to my hacking abilities, we'd been able to study the blueprints of the building, so we knew the general direction of where to look.

"Okay ladies, time to go. Alpha team, move out."

I tapped my comm unit. "Alpha team moving out."

I listened as Noah gave instructions for each of the teams to move forward. At that point, we were to go silent on comms unless urgent, each team with their own instructions. Thanks to a little bug I planted in the security systems of the warehouse, the side door opened with no problems.

Oskar shook his head. "Remind me never to piss you off. I have a feeling I'd be light some euros if you ever got near my bank account."

I just rolled my eyes as I worked the panel and got the door open. After I tucked the panel inside a compartment in my vest, I palmed both my guns and got ready for action.

We took the long, dark hallway and veered left. Rafe went right. I had a feeling that they had given me a babysitter. Further down, the hallway branched, and off Oskar went.

I avoided the cameras, heading down the hall and to

the right. Then I went to the series of doorways. They were more like cells really. I tried the doors; none of them gave. Peeking inside, I could see that most of the rooms were just storage or labs. No people. No heat signatures. When I came to the door at the end of the hall, there were heat signatures. And I prayed that I'd hit the jackpot.

I took out my panel one more time and begged the decryption program to run faster. "Please, please, please. Please let her be okay."

When the green lights flashed, I nodded in satisfaction and tucked it back inside my vest. Guns at the ready, I let myself in.

As I crept in, someone behind me screeched like a banshee and jumped me. It took me less than a second to realize the person trying to go for my guns was no trained killer.

Small, slight, and feminine.

I subdued her easily and had her on the ground, on her back, while I gently cradled her head to push her down. And then I went to the chair. But the person on the chair stood and raised the chair up above her head, ready to wield it like a weapon.

"Gemma, it's me, Matthias."

She hesitated. "What?"

"It's me, love. Love, I came for you."

For what seemed like a long stretch of several seconds, she held the chair over her head, and then I could see her start to shake.

"Hush now. Hush." I re-holstered one of my weapons and reached out for her, gently stroking a thumb over her cheek. "See? It's me. You can put the chair down."

She closed her eyes briefly before lowering the chair. Then she threw herself at me.

"Hey. Hey, you're okay. I've got you now." It was only when she sobbed into my neck that I let some of the emotions start to take over. I wanted to hold her, nuzzle into her scent, and relish the thought that I had her. But I knew that I had to get her out and get her to safety.

"Come on, love, we have to go." I took one of my weapons from my ankle holster and handed it to her. "If anybody moves in a way you don't like, point this and shoot. Let's go."

She shook her head. "Wait, I have to find Sabine."

My gaze swung back to the woman who was still lying on the floor, rubbing her sternum where I'd hit her. "That's Sabine?"

Gemma nodded. "Yeah, we were lying in wait for one of the guards."

Was it bad that I was really excited that she wasn't just waiting for me to come and save her? That was hot.

"I love you. You know that."

She grinned. "I love you too."

"Let's go. Come on, Sabine. We have to move quickly, yeah?"

"I don't know if I can keep up." Sabine's voice was breathy.

Gemma was having none of it though. "You'll make it. Come on, I've got you." She wound Sabine's arm around her shoulder and blinked wide dark eyes at me. "Let's go. I'll carry her all the way if I have to. But we're not leaving her. Not this time."

That hit me right in the little bit of conscience I had left, so I nodded. Then we were on the move, me in the front while the girls followed behind. Quickly, I tapped my watch three times to send the signal that I had them and was moving out. I didn't speak. It was unlikely that anyone was listening in on our channel, but why take the risk?

Silently, I led them through the dim hallways, always going first around every corner, using palm mirrors. Sabine managed to keep up with Gemma's help; she was tough. Gemma wasn't screwing around either. She had her gun constantly at the ready even though it had to be difficult for her to move while holding Sabine's weight. But she did it. I silently counted how many hallways we'd have to go. I'd made four turns. We were down to two. And then I heard the first splintering of concrete above my head.

"Bollocks. We have company." None of my guns had silencers on them, but clearly, someone didn't want to make a loud noise and ruckus.

I was on comms in a second. "Shots fired. I could use some backup. South entrance. Two turns." After I gave the relative position, I fired two shots into the hallway. Gemma fired as well. I palmed another gun and handed it over to her.

I looked at Sabine and said, "Are you okay? Can you manage this? Can you fire a gun?"

She shook her head. "No, I've never fired a gun."

Another set of shots rang out. This time, one whizzing by my ear so close it felt like kiss of fire along my face. "Move." We ran while shooting, returning fire, ducking behind and inside doorways for cover. Gemma ran out of ammo first. I handed her a clip, which she efficiently released and inserted, and then she fired again. No questions, no qualms.

When we were home, I was definitely going to have her play out the Black Widow fantasy. The woman was just plain sexy.

I fired another exploratory shot down the hallway. "Let's move."

"I can run on my own. Let's go," Sabine muttered

and tossed Gemma's arm off of her shoulder. "Go. Come on, let's move."

I ran ahead, as now we had company from both sides. Gemma had our back. Sabine was trying to stay in the doorway as we laid down cover fire. When we ran and made our turn to the hallway, I was first. We had a lot of company.

I tapped my comm unit again. "Mates, where the fuck are you?"

Rafe's voice muttered in my ear, "We have company here too. On our way."

On the line came Dylan's voice. "We have the vehicle. Going to your location."

Thank fuck.

"All right. Round the corner, out the door. Run like hell. Dylan's waiting for you. Don't look back." As we ran, the next thing I heard was a fall along with a *crack! Crack!*

Behind me, Gemma turned. "No, Sabine!" She immediately halted her steps and tried to go back, but I dragged her with me.

"No. No going back. Move."

She fought me. "I have to go back for her. I can't leave her."

"I'm sorry, love." I didn't have time for arguing. I bent and scooped Gemma up and tossed her over my shoulder. Once I had her where she couldn't run back, I fired a gun to the left, hitting my target, who went down with a soft thud fifty feet from the door. To the right, I hit another target. This one groaned and tried to feebly raise his gun. I fired again, and then he was down for good.

Over my shoulder, Gemma pleaded, "Put me down, you asshole. I have to go back."

Oh, she was going to be mad at me. But I didn't care. All I had to do was get her to safety. Once I was out the door, the bright sunlight temporarily blinded me. Right outside the door, Rafe and Oskar were waiting for us. I handed Gemma off, fully intending to go back for Sabine, but there was too much fire. Rafe shook his head at me.

"No go."

"Fuck. Bugger. Bollocks." We had enemy fire on all sides. And all of us had to fire as we ran for the van. Oskar was nicked in the shoulder but kept on moving as if he hadn't even been touched.

Once we were in the van, we did a quick count off to make sure we had all our people, and then Dylan peeled out of there.

For five minutes, we drove like the devil was chasing us out of the warehouse area and then into Chiswick proper. We made lefts, and then gut-tossing rights over the small, pinched side streets into the garage.

Dylan swung the car into an empty spot in the lower level. We all spilled out, heading to our respective cars. When Gemma didn't move right away, I took her hand and she snatched it back. She climbed out of the van on her own accord.

"You bastard."

"Gemma, we can do this later. As soon as you get to the hotel, we'll come up with another plan. We'll go back for her. But I couldn't—"

She slapped me hard across the face. The stinging crack across my cheek made all the worse because she knew how to throw a hit. I didn't react.

After all, you deserve it, don't you?

She was right. You left her friend to die. Just like all those years ago.

"Gems—"

She hit me again. This time her punch was wild as she threw her whole body into it. I merely deflected and then she was sobbing and staggering back. I went for her, but then Rafe stepped between us. "No. Let her go. She'll ride with us."

"What the fuck? I need to talk to her." Oskar got between us and then Ryan and Dylan. I stepped back. "You really think after everything that I could hurt her?"

Oskar shrugged. "Well, when you go all stabby, you know..."

Dylan shook his head. "Dude, too soon."

Oskar just shrugged. "You say that like I'm the one who stabbed someone."

I ignored them, and my gaze met Gemma's. "I wouldn't hurt you."

She shoved through the guys and met my gaze with a lifted chin. "I'm not afraid of him, you assholes. I'm pissed. And frankly, I can't be around any of you right now."

As we all climbed in our respective cars, I had no choice but to watch her walk away.

14

___

Gemma

I HEARD the door to the bedroom open sometime after I'd taken a shower and thrown on an oversized T-shirt. Noah had put us all up in a massive townhouse in Mayfair. Was this one of the Blake Security safe houses?

At first, Matthias didn't say anything, but I could feel his presence in the doorway. It was as if my whole body went into hyperalert mode. Right down to the cellular level, everything woke the hell up.

He said nothing at first. Just unstrapped all his personal weapons and started putting them away into the gun safe along the wall, near the bookshelves. Just like the penthouse, there was the armory with all the extra-fancy weapons, extra ammo and more guns than the guys probably knew what to do with. But each of the rooms was also equipped with a safe.

I knew I owed him an apology. I'd wanted to say it as soon as I'd gone crazy on him, but it had hurt too much. I loved him. He needed to know that.

While his back was still turned, I approached him warily. "I shouldn't have hit you. I'm sorry."

I could see his broad shoulders move up and down as if he was inhaling deep, then exhaling. His voice was soft when he spoke. "I couldn't let you go after her, Gems. I—I wouldn't have survived if something had happened to you. You are my directive. I only care if *you* live or die. That's it. I need you to understand that I will protect you first and foremost, and I won't be sorry about that."

I swallowed hard. "I understand. I just—I made her a promise and seeing her go down then not being allowed to do anything... I just felt like I was failing her. I'm afraid of what they might be doing to her."

"I'm sorry. But I can't allow you to be in danger, not even to save an old friend. No one will ever take priority over you. Right or wrong, it's just never happening."

"Matthias..." The first sob tore out of my throat.

"You're right. I know you're right. It was tactically a better move. I reacted emotionally."

He finally turned around, but I couldn't read his expression. His gorgeous face was a mask. "You can't do that. I'm unstable as fuck. This is what scares me."

What? No. I shook my head. "I'm not afraid of you. You would never hurt me. Not again. That wasn't you before."

His lips set in a tight line. "Tell that to Noah."

I tipped my chin up and met his gaze. "I'm different."

His jaw clenched. "Doesn't matter if you are. You are taking a risk with me."

He was not doing this. I wasn't going to let him crawl back into his shell. "I'm not afraid of you. I believe in you enough for the both of us. I was angry, and I shouldn't have lashed out, because it was an asshole thing to do to the person you love, not because I need to be afraid of you. I'm not letting you push me away."

In the next second, he closed the distance between us and bracketed me against the wall with his hands. "Why can't you just do the thing that's safer for you?" His eyes darkened, and he growled. "But I can't let you go. Even if I know it's better for you. Don't ever scare me like that again."

Before I knew it, before I could even respond or mentally prepare, his lips were crushing mine.

Holy shit. Matthias tasted so good. He wasn't as practiced as some guys, but he was pure raw passion and singed my nerve endings with every stroke of his tongue.

After the initial crush of his lips, he softened, gentled. He teased, probed, waited for me to respond, waited for me to allow him in... or push him away. As if there was any chance that was happening.

He had a subtle way of flooding my senses. It was mere seconds before I was melting, leaning into him, wanting more, craving more.

Before I knew it, my hands were sliding up to his pecs, and I was clutching on to his T-shirt. Under the soft cotton, he was all hard muscle and carved stone. When my nails dug in a little, he growled low and shoved one hand into my hair, gripping and angling my head just how he wanted as he took long licks into my mouth, leaving no corner unexplored.

His body pressed into mine, forcing me to arch my back if I didn't want it pressed into the wall. Of course, that motion made my breasts press against him more. My nipples were tight, my skin too hot. And Jesus Christ, I could feel the thick length of him throbbing against my belly as if begging to come home. As if letting me know we were just getting started.

With another muffled groan, he lifted me, forcing my legs to wrap around his hips so that his steel-like erection pressed against my center. Pressing into that spot I desperately needed the most.

It was like he was reaching deep inside me, stroking every single pleasure center simultaneously.

He made little teasing licks and would act as if he was withdrawing. And then I'd whimper, or instinctively follow the source of my pleasure, and he would give a harsh chuckle, before delving in for more.

Before I even knew what the hell was happening, I felt a tingling electricity over my skin, as if all my synapses were firing at once. The heat built in my core until I was on the edge of eruption. The tingle started in the base of my spine and I leaned into it. Leaned into every sensation, every touch, every lick.

I slid my hands into his hair, scoring his scalp with my fingernails. And he shuddered just before growling low. He tucked a hand under my T-shirt, sliding over my belly, stopping just under the edge of my breast.

Oh God yes. I wanted his hands on me. I needed him to affirm that we were okay, that I was still his and he was still mine.

All I wanted were his hands.

Matthias

ALL I WANTED to do was touch her. Just get a small taste before I stopped. *Can you stop? Can you stop what's happening?* The truth was I didn't know because she tasted like heaven. And who was I kidding? I'd already told her I couldn't give her up. She was my anchor. So, selfish as it was, I wasn't letting her go. Not now, not ever.

I'd been riding on the edge of madness since the warehouse. I had a serious desire to give her a good and proper spanking for trying to risk her life and then for losing her shit with me. I only had a tenuous control on who I was. She couldn't take risks like that. But fuck it, I'd rather be inside her.

Sliding my hands up the nape of her neck, I gently stroked her cheek as I kissed her. Why did she taste so good? There was a hint of sweetness to her lips that reminded me of the strawberries she always smelled like.

Every stroke of my tongue was met with one of hers and sent a shiver through me. When Gemma rolled her hips, she slid right over my rock-hard erection, making me groan. With every gasp and moan, she silently pleaded for more. And I wanted to give it to her.

The angel on my shoulder warned me we needed

more talking. But the devil was riding me and telling me all the things I wanted to hear. *Just give her one orgasm, then you can talk.* In my lust-fogged brain, this sounded like a fantastic idea.

I dragged my lips from hers and kissed along her jaw then nuzzled her neck. "You smell fucking incredible."

When I moved my hand up her thigh, my fingers met the edge of her panties and they were soaked. *Jesus.* My dick throbbed, and I gritted my teeth against the wave of lust. *Take. Taste. Mark.*

I slid my fingers under the elastic of her panties, rolling my thumb over her clit. Her whole body shook, and she threw her head back.

With a low, muttered curse she planted one leg on the shelf of the opposite bookcase. She tore her lips from mine and groaned. "Oh my God. Yes ... right ... there."

I watched her face carefully as I rubbed a slow, gentle circle over her clit. Her mouth hung open as she worked her hips into my touch. Jesus, she was beautiful. I wanted more from her. Carefully, I added a finger, slowly sliding inside her with a gentle retreat. Gemma bit her bottom lip.

"You are so soft," I whispered, adding a second finger. Her eyes popped open and she blinked rapidly, but I didn't gentle the caress. It wasn't until I curved my fingers and found that bundle of nerves inside, pressing gently, that she broke apart.

I dropped my forehead to hers. "That's it Gemma. Give it to me." And I stroked her inside over and over again.

"I–Jesus. I'm going..." She bowed her body, and I watched in awe while her pussy clamped around my fingers. *Oh yeah.* This was what I wanted to see. Gemma open and completely out of control. I fucking loved it. I wanted to make her do it again.

Gently easing my fingers from her, I brought them to my lips. She tasted incredible. "That's good, love."

"I want more," she pleaded. She was far from done with me, and she reached for my belt buckle.

I shook my head. "Gemma. You're playing with fire."

"So only you get to tease and torture me? I don't get to do the same to you?"

I blinked hard, trying to bring my brain back online. Gemma slid her hands inside my cargos, and I was lost. Her delicate fingers wrapped around me and then she pumped once. Twice. The third time my knees buckled.

I choked out, "Fuck, Gemma!"

She flushed. "I've been picturing doing this to you."

Where in the world had she been hiding my whole life? "I love how you think."

Between her words, the need I saw in her eyes, and

the way her thumb stroked over the tip of my cock and then gently stroked the underside of the tip, I couldn't wait. My gaze never left hers. Through clenched teeth I asked, "You sure you want this?"

Gemma nodded. "I need it."

I cupped her ass, lifting her until I nudged her gently before kissing her again. I shoved her knickers aside and guided my cock to her slick, heated core. *Oh fuck*. If I did this, she would own me. But I didn't give a fuck.

Her eyes widened with surprise, and then she locked onto my gaze again and relaxed.

The second she did that, I sank deep and we both hissed. *Shit*. My eyes crossed. I was never leaving. She pulsed around me and I swore I could stay inside Gemma forever.

She dug her nails into my shoulders, and my name was a whisper on her tongue. With each slide and retreat, my knees weakened. Gemma placed her hand above her using one of the shelves for more leverage as I fucked her.

My gaze occasionally dipped to where we were joined, watching my cock slide in and out of her. When she arched her back, I dipped my head to draw one of her nipples into my mouth.

"I. Yes. Harder. Oh God. Oh my God."

Against her nipple I muttered, "Quiet, love. The walls in this house are thin."

Her response was to tug on my hair, and I couldn't help the soft chuckle. I loved the sounds she made, but I didn't want Oskar being an arsehole to her tomorrow with his knowing looks.

Later, I'd focus on her breasts. I had plans for them. I wanted to take my time licking them, kissing them, biting them—fucking them, like I'd seen at the club. It was an image I hadn't been able to get out of my head.

When I felt the quiver of her pussy around my dick, I knew she was close. I snapped my hips, and her eyes went wide. To help her along, I worked a hand between us and found her sensitive clit. My first touch was gentle, but then I stroked more firmly.

"That's it. Come for me. I'm addicted to the sight."

My eyes crossed as her slick walls clamped around my dick and milked me. *Jesus Christ. So tight.* She felt so good. With three more pumps, I was coming apart as my control fell away.

All that was left of me in the end were the shattered pieces she left. I felt stripped bare as I clutched on to her.

Another orgasm rolled through her and she tightened around me once more. By that point, all I could do was groan as she rode out the wave.

Holy fuck.

I kissed her again, licking into her mouth even as I slicked my thumb over her clit. Good Lord, it was impossible to think at all when I did that.

With a growl, I carried her to the bed, kicking off my cargos as I went. Her T-shirt went next. I may or may not have accidentally torn her knickers as we fell on top of each other.

I dragged her on top of me then threw my head back into the pillows and cursed low, my hand digging into her hips. "Jesus, fuck me."

Gemma chuckled. "I think I'm getting to that... again"

She slid both hands over my skin and then used her thumb to spread the drop of liquid that pooled at the tip of my dick again. "I think he likes me."

Jesus, I was going to die from pleasure. I'd managed to keep myself alive for all these years, but fucking Gemma was going to put me down. "I think that's pretty obvious."

"I like how you feel," she whispered as I pushed myself further into her hands.

When I spoke, my voice was strained, more of a low growl really. "I love how you make me feel."

Her thumb toyed with my piercing and my brows knit, but my hips rocked upwards, pushing myself further into her hands. "Please don't fucking stop. Bloody fucking amazing."

Gemma raised a brow. "You like it when I play with this?" Gently she ran her fingers over the thin, silver ring again and a shudder wracked my body.

One of my hands finally released her hip and slid up her torso, stroking my thumb over her nipple through the lace of her bra. "What do you think?"

I smirked. "I got it because of the pain. I didn't know the practical application of pleasure really. When you touch it—fuck—I could come just from that. Maybe it's like when I do this." I ran my thumb over her nipple and relished how her eyes rolled back into her head. "I love how responsive you are. One day soon, I want to see if you can come from me doing nothing else but this. Just pinching your nipples, licking them, biting them."

She shivered. "I want that, too." She raised herself up on her knees and positioned me at her cleft. One hand stroking down to the root of my cock, she held me still before gently swiveling her hips. Coating the tip of me.

"Jesus, Gemma. Fuck a twat." My hips rocked into her. The first inch of me slid inside her easily.

She threw her head back and held perfectly still. "I think I can come just like this. You make me feel so full, so stretched."

"Jesus. Fuck, you feel good," I mumbled then pinched her nipple harder.

Gemma gasped, and her pussy clamped around my dick like a vise. "I. God you feel so—"

I shoved a hand into her hair and gripped tight. She licked her lips before biting down and rocking her hips a little bit more, taking more of me inside her. "This feels so much better without the condoms."

I panted, sliding in just a little bit more and then retreating an inch. The glide and pressure made me tingle. "Gemma..." Fuck, I was going to come again. I gripped her hips, my fingertips pressing deep into her skin as I slid all the way home and watched intently where we were joined. As I made love to her, I muttered words of need and longing and love. I told her, in all the ways I could, how I felt.

Gemma arched and leaned back so she could brace herself on my knees. That new position gave me all the access I needed.

I lifted up then leaned over her body, sucking one stiff nipple into my mouth, and groaned against her breast. My other hand slid between our bodies, pressing slow, easy circles on her clit.

She was coming in seconds, flying high and clamping around my dick. But I wasn't done. I kept going, snapping my hips forward and making her gasp and widen her eyes when I hit that magical place deep inside her. And then I would retreat. With each snap of my hips, she screamed my name. So much for keeping quiet. But fuck them. I'd had to endure their sexcapades for years.

As her orgasm coursed through her, sending her body into wicked convulsions, I growled and pulled her forward on my lap. I slid my lips over hers and pressed my tongue into her mouth, kissing her deep. The top of her pelvis rubbed along mine, prolonging the pleasure and the hit of ecstasy.

Gemma held tight onto my shoulders as I kissed her, her hips still working, her body still taking me deep. This was perfection.

I dragged my lips off of hers and kissed along her jaw, whispering to her, making her hotter. "So fucking beautiful... I could do this all damn day... You feel so good..." My hand fisted in her hair more gently than before, while the other slid over her ass, rocking her more firmly against me as I loved her.

Then I tried something I'd seen at the club. Gently, slowly, in case she didn't like it. When I slid a finger down the seam of her ass, she hesitated for only a moment but then relaxed against me.

When my finger pressed against her pucker, she tossed her head back. "Oh God." But when I eased a finger gently inside, she broke apart again, pushing herself up onto her knees and slamming back down over me.

I held perfectly still, my muscles going rigid. As I came, my gaze didn't leave hers, and I sank home one more time. "I am never letting you go. We belong together."

Gemma sank over me once more, and we both groaned, riding the wave of the last vestiges of our orgasms.

15
———

Gemma

THE SOUND of a phone ringing filtered through my dreams. It took a second but then my brain came online all at once when I registered the ringtone.

My burner phone was ringing.

I shot out of bed, almost falling in my haste to get to my duffel bag. When we'd first got here, I dumped all my stuff in the corner. I figured I wouldn't be needing it anymore.

By the time I got to the phone, my breath was coming fast, and I'd broken a nail.

"Hello," I gasped into the receiver, hoping that the

caller wouldn't hang up.

"I'm disappointed in you, Gemma. I thought you'd be different."

The sound of Father's voice coming over the line made me wake up instantly. My heart sank. If Father was calling me directly something was wrong.

"What do you want?" It probably wasn't wise to speak to him that way, but I was so far gone, I didn't care.

I could tell by the change in his voice that he didn't appreciate my attitude. "We don't trust you anymore. You can't follow simple instructions. So we're coming to you tomorrow. Bring Matthias, or Sabine dies."

The line went dead.

"No, wait!"

But it was too late; he was already gone. I hit the button to hang up and dropped the phone on the bed. I hated to wake Matthias, but he would know what to do. I was done trying to handle the situation on my own. If there was anything I'd learned through this whole process it was that we had to stick together.

"Matthias? Wake up." I rocked his shoulder gently until his eyes opened. He looked around frantically until he noticed me sitting on the bed next to him. His shoulders lowered in relief.

"Gemma? What's going on? What happened?"

After all our time together, he could tell by the look on my face that something was wrong.

"They're going to kill Sabine. Father just called."

He sat up and pushed the covers down. "Slow down. When did he call?"

"Just now." I pointed to the burner phone. I didn't trust myself to speak anymore. I was already on the verge of tears.

"Hold on," Matthias said as he climbed out of bed. He crossed the room and picked up his laptop. For the next few minutes, there was only the sound of his fingers tapping on the keys. Then he cursed.

"Dammit. I thought we might be able to trace it."

I shook my head. "They've always insisted on burner phones. Even when they trusted me."

His head fell down to his arms. "Yeah, I was just hoping we'd catch a break. I'm worried about what they'll do if we don't give them what they want."

Something about the way he was talking made me nervous. "What do you mean give them what they want? That's not possible."

His eyes lifted, and when I saw the look on his face my blood chilled. "No way. Matthias, you can't be thinking—"

He stood up and came to sit on the bed next to me. When he reached over to take my hand, I snatched it back. He wasn't going to sweet-talk me into agreeing to whatever crazy plan he was currently formulating.

"Every moment that we delay, her life is in danger. We know what they want. Me."

"We can't give them you. *I need you.*"

His eyes flashed. "I know you do, baby. But this is the only way we can save Sabine."

Unable to sit still while we talked about offering him up like a lamb to slaughter, I jumped off the bed and paced the floor.

"Do you understand what you're saying? They're not inviting you to tea, Matthias. They want to kill you."

"And they won't succeed," he said with maddening certainty. "They have no idea what they're up against. Blake Security will plan and execute the entire operation. With Noah, Rafe, and the other guys watching out for me, I'll be as safe as possible. It's the best chance we have to get Sabine back."

"But there's no mission that's 100 percent safe. You and I both know that."

He didn't bother to deny it. We were ORUS agents. No one understood how fleeting life could be better than we did. But it didn't change the look on his face. It was a look I knew well. He wasn't going to change his mind.

"You're really going to do this, huh?"

He stood up. "I am. If this is what it takes, then this is what I'll do." For moment he looked pensive. "She was my friend, too."

In that moment, I felt terrible. The entire time I'd been operating as though the mission to save Sabine had nothing to do with him. It was something that mattered to me. But he was completely right. Sabine wasn't just my friend. Matthias grew up with her, too. He had just as much of a right to want to save her as I did.

"So what are we going to do?"

Now he looked smug. "Exactly what I said. Give them what they want. Me."

"But there has to be more to it than just that. We can't just drop you off and expect them to give Sabine up."

He looked me in the eye. "We aren't going to do this lightly. I hope you know that. We're all going to work to make things as safe as possible. Trust me."

"I do trust you. I hope you know that. I'm just not ready to trust that the universe is on our side in this."

He took me in his arms and for that moment everything was calm. I wished that we could stay there forever where nothing could harm us. But we would have to be separated eventually.

"I guess we should go talk to the guys then?"

Now he looked worried. "They might already be working on this plan."

I sighed. "Of course they are."

He looked sheepish. "I didn't want to waste any time."

"I get it." And I did. Every moment that we delayed made it more likely that Sabine wouldn't still be alive. But it didn't mean that I wasn't going to worry.

"There are so many things that could go wrong. What if they don't give her back? What if you get hurt?"

"I won't. We'll be ready. Hell, by the time we're done, they'll wish they could give me back."

Matthias

EVEN THOUGH THIS whole thing was my plan, I was starting to have serious second thoughts. Gemma stood in front of Oskar as he helped her put on a lightweight, bullet-resistant vest.

My mind was stuck on the word *resistant*. We couldn't put her in full battle gear. She was supposed to look like she was unarmed. But everything inside of me wished that we could cover her in bubble wrap.

The idea of sending her out into the world unprotected made me crazy. Putting myself in danger was one thing, but not her. Never her. A small part of me wondered how I was going to handle her going out on ORUS missions in the future. I wasn't sexist. I knew there were tons of extremely capable female agents. But that didn't mean I wanted her to be one of them. What I wanted was for her to be safe.

Good luck with that.

Nothing about our life had ever been safe. From the moment she had shown up with the Family, she'd always been one step ahead of danger. And I had to admit that she found her way out of it on her own for the most part. It was a hard thing to admit that she didn't really need me. But I wanted her to need me.

I also wanted Oskar to take his hands off her breasts.

"Okay, okay. I can do that," I grumbled as I knocked his hands away.

He smirked and moved over to the ammunition. I was surprised he didn't make a smart comment, but all the guys seem to be giving me a wide berth today. Maybe I had been a little crankier than usual, but what guy wouldn't be when he was sending the love of his life into the lion's den?

They didn't know what the Family was like, what they were truly capable of. I did, up close and personal. Reading it in a report wasn't the same as living it. It was taking everything inside of me to allow her to walk back in there. Especially knowing that the last time we'd both been there, we'd both almost died.

"You remember the plan?"

She nods. "We've gone over it a million times."

"I know." My hands shook slightly as I adjusted her shirt over the vest. The material was so thin that you couldn't even tell it was there. Exactly what we wanted. "I'm just worried about you."

She scoffed. "Worried about me? I'm going to be safe with Diana the whole time. We'll be in and out before they even know what's happening. You're the one we should be worried about. It's not too late to call this off, you know."

"I'm not calling it off. Let's just focus on getting through this."

The next hour was spent getting ready for the op. Gemma watched as we gathered weapons and went over the plan a final time. The blueprint of the drop-off point was burned into my brain at that point. But Gemma paid close attention, her eyes following as Noah's fingers moved over the screen of his tablet.

Before I knew what was happening, we were in the

car on the way. I wanted to say something to her, but my mind was blank. What did you say to someone when there's a chance the words might be your last?

"I love you."

She smiled. "I love you, too. This has to work."

"The guys are right behind us," I said, reminding her that Noah and Rafe were on our tail. "Dylan and Ryan went ahead to scout out the location." I wasn't sure if the reminders made her feel any better, but they helped me to remember who had my back. The last time I was facing off against the Family, I was a scared teenager with no idea how I would survive in the world and few friends to my name. Now things were different. That was what I had to cling to.

Gemma sighed. "I'm scared."

"I know. But it'll all be over soon." I reached over and grabbed her hand as we drove the rest of the way. Once we approached the drop-off point, I pulled to the side of the road and parked. A black sedan was across the street. The windows were so dark that you couldn't see inside. After a few minutes the door opened, and someone got out.

"Showtime." I leaned over and kissed her. I pretended I didn't feel the moisture against my face.

"I'll see you soon. Be careful." Gemma put a soft

hand to my cheek and the tender touch was almost my undoing.

"Always." I climbed out of the car and walked to the middle of the street. It was deserted, but I knew that Noah and Rafe had eyes on me. It should have given me confidence, but something inside of me was blaring a warning. On the surface, everything was going according to plan, but somehow things felt *off*.

"I'm here. You got what you want. Where's the girl?"

The man facing me was a little older, with dark hair and a small scar on his forehead. I took in all the details in case I needed them later. Although I wasn't stupid enough to think they'd sent anyone but a low-level player to retrieve me.

"We'll take you to the girl. As long as you cooperate."

Another man climbed out of the car. I resisted the urge to fight back as they pushed me toward the back seat. The second goon produced a zip tie and my hands were bound in front of me. But I really only started second-guessing things when they pulled out the black bag.

"Don't worry," Goon Number One said with a smile. "That's for later."

I kept my face impassive, but all I was thinking was, *Noah, don't let me down.*

16

Gemma

"ONCE AGAIN, I want everyone in the bleachers to hear me. No one's being a hero today. Alpha team, do you copy?"

I knew Noah was talking to me. He mentioned it to make sure it sank in. I scowled as I slid my gaze to Diana and Rafe, who had the good sense to look elsewhere. Dylan, like an idiot, grinned at me. I just deepened my scowl. "Yes, Alpha team copies. Honestly, you try and rescue a friend one time..."

Rafe's chuckle was low as he checked his weapons.

"Yeah well, I tried to kill people this one time; you'd be amazed how they never let that shit go."

I had gotten some of the story already, but I hadn't really gotten the whole thing. Oskar insisted that it needed acting out.

"Beta team, do you copy?"

Oskar and Ryan acknowledged that they copied. And then Noah asked Charlie team.

Ian's voice came clear on the line. "Charlie team copies."

I understood what needed to happen. I was going to go in with Diana. She was the one who was going to watch those six and guard them at the end of the hall. Rafe was going to stay at the door to make sure no one else came in and no one else went out. Oskar and Ryan were watching egress routes and Ian's team was split, half on Matthias, half as cavalry. Obviously, Noah was on comms. This was a good plan, a very good plan. And we were going to get Sabine, which was the part I liked the most.

"Alpha team, move out." Rafe was the one who handled this hack. He had one of Matthias's decryption devices programmed for us.

After several seconds, the light bulb turned green and disengaged. Then Diana and I, weapons in hand, were on our way. I led the way with Diana not far behind. As far as missions went, this was the kind of thing I pictured as first mission, not deep cover. I thought I'd be going in for rescues and stuff.

This stuff with the Family, I hated everything about it, but this, this felt more like it. As we moved in a modified formation, we made a sharp turn and moved as silently as ninjas. Our feet barely made any sound. When we reached the end of the main hallway, Dylan tapped Diana on the shoulder, and Diana tapped me. He signaled this was the end of his road, and he was going to watch our backs as we went forward. Luckily, from the blueprints we had been shown of the old warehouse in Walthamstow where Matthias and I had grown up, it hadn't changed much. Some modernization was made two years ago, but only on the portion that contained the offices and residence of Father.

If that's where he even lives anymore.

But the rest of the facility remained largely unchanged, including where they normally kept prisoners.

When we reached a blind hallway, we halted when Noah spoke into the comms. "Alpha team hold. Enemy at your two o'clock walking toward a T-junction off your hallway."

I held my breath, beads of sweat popping on my brow, forcing myself to remember my training. With each breath I inhaled, I counted to three, held, counted to three, exhaled, counted to three.

As we stood there waiting and listening for any hint of a sound, it seemed that Diana was doing the same thing. Had she been trained? I knew she wasn't ORUS, but from what I understood, Diana trained with the guys on hand-to-hand and weapons. I had first assumed that she was just Rafe's fiancée. I never thought that Diana worked for Blake Security as well.

One. Two. Three. In.

One. Two. Three. Out.

In and out, we both timed our breaths, staying as relaxed as possible while poised on the razor edge of a machete.

Finally, Noah's voice came back over the comms. "All clear. Move forward."

As if we hadn't had to cope with standing stock-still for the last three minutes, we sprang into action with the fluidity of a sword master. We moved forward and headed toward that hallway. I held up my left hand, pointing down the hall, signaling toward the window. Diana acknowledged the signal, and then we moved forward, carefully avoiding the window.

It was only when we'd almost passed the room on the left that I saw the lock of blond hair through the corner of my eye. I gave the immediate *hold* command.

When I turned for a better look, I saw Sabine in a chair, with her back to the window and door. Why the hell wasn't she kept with the rest of the prisoners? No matter.

I signaled for the decryption keypad and placed it on the door. This door had less security than the external doors. In a matter of seconds, the light turned green. Weapon raised, I turned the handle and moved silently inside with Diana on my heels, watching my back.

Sabine didn't even turn around. Instead she muttered, "Are they dead yet?"

Diana stared, quickly checking for guards, but there was nothing. The room was... comfortable. Sabine was in some kind of armchair, facing the television. On the left was a table with snacks. Next to it was a refrigerator. The floor was carpeted and worn, but most importantly, Sabine wasn't tied up.

I raised my gun. "Just what the fuck is going on?"

My friend whipped around, blond locks flying, and then sighed when she saw us. "Is this the part where I pretend you rescued me?"

———

Matthias

Whose bright idea was this again? Oh yeah, mine.

It was killing me to not fight back. But this was for Gemma. I owed her. And I'd made her promises. Ones I intended to keep.

We pulled up in the middle of an unfamiliar area. It could have been basically anywhere in East London, or South London for that matter.

There were warehouses all around. I was dragged out of the car roughly and then shoved out onto the street. "Easy gents. You don't want to rough up the merchandise," I mumbled. That only earned me another shove forward.

I had to blink rapidly to adjust to the sunlight, and I tried to rotate my shoulders as much as I could to accommodate for the zip ties on my hands.

"Any one of you fuckwits want to tell me which way we're going?"

One of the guys, the short, stocky one on the left, shoved me slightly. "Shut it."

"Sorry, mate. I'm just trying to make conversation." And also to stall. I didn't know how much time Gemma was going to need. But from what I'd figured, the longer I could stall the better.

"The only conversation you'll be having is with Father, so shut your trap."

"Interesting you should say that. I've been looking forward to speaking with him."

"Well, I doubt you'll be so happy about it when he gets his hands on you. Do you know how long we've been meaning to kill you?"

I chuckled harshly. "It turns out I'm not that easy to kill. He's tried it once or twice. He's going to fail this time too."

It turned out Stocky and Not Too Bright didn't appreciate that, given he landed a sharp jab to my side. Pain radiated through my kidney as I gritted my teeth, cursing through it.

"Shut it."

"Okay, okay. I hear you. You're too daft to have a challenging conversation with anyway. I'll wait till I'm in the room with the real top dogs. What's it like knowing that you're nothing but a shitty little errand boy?"

Goddamn, another jab. Stocky and Not Too Bright shoved me forward, and around the corner there was another car idling.

What the fuck? This was not the plan. "Oi! What the fuck is this? You're supposed to be taking me to Father now."

"Oh, you'll get to Father." Short and Stocky leaned in and I figured I'd have to add in dragon breath as part of the nickname, too. "He just wants you going on a bit more of an adventure first."

And then it came out. The one thing I'd been hoping they wouldn't do: the bag, right over the head.

I only struggled a little. I hated these things. I'd always hated them. Every time I had to work with some new, cagey agent from another agency, I'd end up with one of these over my head. They never smelled good. Dank, dark, and it reminded me too much of my childhood.

Before they shoved me in the car, they did another sweep for weapons. Up and down one leg, up and down the other, a proper pat down at the back, front, under the arms—all standard stuff. None of the idiots had figured that my belt buckle concealed a knife. And that was lucky for me, because when shit went wrong, and it was bound to at some point, I'd feel at least a little bit better with one of my knives on me.

Of course, I had my smaller comm unit still in. No one had thought to sweep me for bugs. At least it was concealed.

Next thing I knew, my head was being grabbed and I was shoved in the back seat of the second car. Once we were moving, I tried to pay attention and track our route. But it was difficult since we'd stopped amongst all those warehouses. I had no idea where we were. All I could do was trust that my team had an eye on me.

The car was mostly silent as we drove. While I might not have known where we were going, I knew approximately how long we'd been driving. In just short of ten minutes, the driver slammed on the brakes, and I was jostled so far, I nearly went flying into the front seat. All I heard was my comm going off. "Shit, we have trouble."

The only thought I had before I calmly unlocked the gate that contained my monster was... Gemma.

17

Gemma

"Sabine, what the hell are you doing?"

Sabine seemed like she was in no kind of hurry. No sense of urgency. No worry. No fear. "Gemma, I wish I could say I was happy or even surprised to see you, but I'm neither."

Diana tapped on the doorframe. "We gotta get a move on."

I signaled her for one more minute, then turned back to Sabine. "Okay, just get your stuff. Let's go."

"Are you daft?" The venom rolled off Sabine in

waves. "When are you going to get it? I'm not coming with you. As a matter of fact, I'm the bait."

My brows drew down. "What are you talking about? I came back for *you*. You were hurt."

Sabine rolled her eyes. "I wasn't hurt. I tripped on purpose once I realized your man was going to get away. Father only wanted you because he knew it would bring him in. He said you went and fell in love with the mark. Not too bright, are you?"

As the seconds ticked by, realization dawned. Sabine wasn't bound; she wasn't gagged; she wasn't afraid. She was no prisoner. She *was* the bait.

The problem was the moment it sunk in, one of the guards came barreling into the room. He and Diana started fighting over his gun, and he knocked her down. I jumped in and an uppercut sent his head snapping back, his big body staggering back a couple of steps.

I took full advantage and locked on him, digging my left hand into his hair, making a fist with my right, and punching him in the throat. Then I jumped off. He choked and staggered back, flailing, trying to get a foothold. First lesson in fighting: if you couldn't breathe, you couldn't fight. Then I went for the base of his stance. I grabbed him by the ears and pulled his big body forward, right onto my knee. The resounding crunch made my stomach roil, but I didn't even blink. Then I turned, ready to drag Sabine by her hair if I had to, and suddenly, my stomach pitched.

Sabine had a gun to Diana's head. "I really wish you hadn't done that. Now they'll blame me. Why do you always have to do this, act like a goddamn hero?"

"I'm not *acting* like a hero. I thought you were my friend. I wanted to help you."

"I don't need your help."

I shook my head. How had I gotten this all wrong? "Was any of this real? Or did Father know all along that I worked for ORUS?"

Sabine tilted her head up, finger on the trigger. Diana, however, stayed nice and calm, hands up where Sabine could see them, appearing to be no threat.

I knew after seeing Diana in action that she could handle herself just fine. But she wasn't taking any stupid chances.

"Don't look at me like that. You don't know what it's like. You *escaped*. Some of us didn't get to escape. Some of us were sold and returned. Sold again. Returned. That's a life that we can't get back. *You ran*." She spat out those words with venom.

"I was trying to get back to you. Yes, I was assigned to come back here, and I never wanted to, but I had unique knowledge that could help me infiltrate better. Imagine how sick I was to find the same people that I'd left behind were still here, that there were people who never found their way out. And before you start thinking how lucky I was to have escaped, you don't know how I escaped. Those people threw me into the Thames and left me for dead."

Sabine's face fell, her bravado replaced by sadness and sorrow. Her eyes went soft and her mouth turned down, smoothing some of the hard edge. "There is no normal. This is all there is, survival. You're a fool if you've never learned that. You're stupid if after all these years away you thought you could change anything about this place."

There was more shuffling of feet near the door, and I cursed. I heard a guard saying to the mic, "We've been compromised."

I didn't waste any time. I just turned and fired my weapon. One to the chest and one to the head. This wasn't my first kill. I'd killed in all kinds of ways. But this was strangely numbing, as if there were a big, empty hole inside my heart now that I could never fill up because of this one act I'd taken.

When I turned back, I leveled my gun at Sabine. "Let my friend go."

Sabine shook her head. "I wish I lived in your world where something like that might happen."

I shook my head and prayed that Sabine would

listen to me. I prayed that the little girl that once lived inside was still there. "Please do not make me do this. There's a way out of this. You just don't see it yet."

Sabine didn't even blink. "We're all just doing what we have to do."

My finger moved on the trigger, and then every single instinct, every single hour of training, kicked into sheer focus on that point. One wrong move and I would hit Diana, but I wasn't even worried. Much like with the guard, I leveled my gun, fired, and Sabine went down.

It was as if time slowed. The bullet blasted through the air following a precise trajectory and struck Sabine. Her petite body snapped backward and then slowly sank to the ground. I watched it all in horror, pain, and sadness.

I wasn't sure how long I stood there staring, frozen and unable to move, unable to process, but Diana grabbed me by the arm. "Listen to me. We have to get out of here. Move your ass."

But I couldn't. I stared at Sabine. I'd risked Matthias for this. For someone whose love was more memory than reality. Why had I done that?

Because you thought Sabine was like you, and in reality, she wasn't.

The fog lifted momentarily. I let myself be dragged

out by Diana. She tugged me down the hall, watching both our fronts and our backs.

When we rounded the corner toward the main exit point, we found Dylan in the hall engaged in hand-to-hand, and it was getting ugly.

Matthias

GLASS SHATTERED AROUND ME.

The crash had me wincing, and the sound made my ears pop. What the fuck was going on? Where was my team? What was happening? The pain didn't even register yet. All I could think about was this was not according to plan. Something was wrong.

And then I was airborne.

I went into a state of weightlessness that felt like an eternity. It was probably only a second, and then the hard, jarring crash back down. My shoulders roared from my positioning with the zip ties. And all I could do was groan. I was in complete and total darkness. But one sniff told me something either hit the fuel tank or it had ruptured for some reason. Real soon, this car was going to be up in flames. I needed to make sure I didn't become barbecue.

Suddenly, there was some jostling. Cursing. Gunfire. But I remained unharmed and untouched.

Did that cursing sound familiar? What was going on? I wished I could fucking see. Then the next thing I knew I was being hauled out of the car, dragged, and then the zip ties were cut. Someone yanked the bag off of my head.

I squinted to shield my eyes from any light that might be shining in them, but it was still dark, and then a face filled my vision. "You awake now, princess? We got trouble."

I forgot all about my stinging shoulders at that point. And then I tucked one foot under the opposite knee, placed my hands on the shattered glass and popped into fight stance. "What's wrong? Gemma?"

Rafe gave me a terse nod. "I'll fill you in on the way. We're not far from the facility that she broke into. Our guess is they were taking you in the securest way back there in the hopes of losing your tail."

I nodded. "You got my knives?"

Rafe just rolled his eyes. "I'll give you one better."

When we reached the follow car, Rafe reached into the back seat and handed me a full vest, my guns, weapons, grenades—the whole nine. "I think this is better than a few knives."

I nodded my thanks and strapped into my vest and then gave Noah an appreciative nod. "I would hug you, mate. But first, I want to go get my girl."

Noah grinned. "Don't ever say I never gave you nothin'. Let's go."

The ride to the other warehouse was less than a minute. And the whole time my whole body hummed with energy, rage, and violence.

"What the fuck happened? It was supposed to be in and out."

Noah grumbled in the front seat. "Yeah, supposed to be. The best laid plans and all that shit. It turns out, Sabine was not at all friendly. She was in on it the whole time."

I stared at him for a moment. "So you're telling me the whole thing went tits-up because the damsel in distress was no damsel at all."

"Yeah, right. That about sums it up. We're here. You boys go do your thing."

Rafe tapped me on the shoulder and gave Noah a smile of solidarity. "I know, brother. You wish you were in there. But since that one—" He inclined his head toward me. "—went all *Kill Bill* on your ass, it's best to sit this one out, lest Lucia have my ass for getting you killed."

Noah grumbled but said nothing else. His gaze met mine and he said to me, "Go get your girl and bring her home."

"Too right."

I followed Rafe around the corner to our mark for entry. Rafe signaled that we were going on channel two and then indicated I should follow. We checked our weapons one more time and essentially followed the sound of gunshots. Before opening the door, Rafe turned to me. "I know you're all better and shit now, but this isn't the time for that. If you still have access to that guy, the monster they made, let him loose."

"I have every intention of it."

And I had the opportunity to do just that. The moment we were through the doors, we were struck by two guards. Rafe leveled one easily with an elbow uppercut that had the guard's head snapping back, and then Rafe wasted no time popping him in the throat with a silencer.

I was less surgical about it. It still was a clean kill, but instead of using my gun with a silencer, I used my knife. The blood splattered. It didn't even faze me as I stepped over the dead body and kept moving.

Rafe just rolled his eyes. "What is it with you and the knives?"

"When you have a knife in your hand, it requires you to be up close and personal. It requires you to be intimate with someone. It was the only time I ever actually got close to anyone."

"Yeah, that works."

We turned left in the hallway. I knew that we could handle whatever we encountered. The last thing on earth I wanted was for Father and his crew to move Gemma.

If they moved her, I didn't know if we'd ever be able to find her again. I would move heaven and hell and let the Family know I was coming, but they would relish torturing me, if they could.

It wasn't long until we found Dylan attempting to hold off ten guards. The kid was doing well, but he was outmanned and soon to be outgunned. Rafe tapped him on the shoulder and he nodded his acknowledgement that we were there. Then Rafe turned his attention to me. "Let's do our thing."

I nodded and then promptly tuned out everybody and everything except for the targets in front of me. Rafe went left, I went right. Dylan kept firing shots and laying cover for us.

The first guy approached and made his first move. I

swept my right arm along his left and then twisted at his wrist. There was a yell of pain and the guy dropped to his knees. Then, I grabbed him by the hair, delivered a knee strike, and popped him in the head with my gun.

As soon as that guy was down, I sheathed my gun again and went for the next. Two guys attacked me at once, hand to hand. That was more difficult, but I just focused on the one on my right and went for the jabs.

The other guy fought back, and I felt each of his blocks. Hammer fist block one, elbow block two, shielding the side of his face as I aimed a hook punch.

But that left my opponent open because the dumbass didn't have his other hand up. Before he could even react, I had my thumbs in his eye sockets. He yowled and tossed his head back, exposing his throat, which I exploited by punching him hard.

The guy choked back his pain, and then I added insult to injury by putting an arm bar across his trachea and using my left arm to hold his right arm nice and steady. Then I delivered a series of knees before finally, fully turning my body to block his friend. When I delivered another sharp knee to the groin, the guy sagged in my arms. Then I let go of his trachea, pulled out my gun and popped him once between the eyes, and then his friend right behind him. "What do you know? Two for the price of one."

I felt rather than heard the next attacker coming from behind down the corridor. But as I turned to face him and fight, the guy went down like a sack of bricks. I shifted my gaze to Dylan, and he nodded.

I gave him a chin nod and headed back on the fray. Two more assailants. Elbows, knees, kicks—a knee to the inner groin and I could almost feel the tear of his muscle. But I was still moving. Still up. A bullet grazed my thigh, and then I let out the monster. I finally unleashed the control and let him at it.

If anyone had asked me later what had happened exactly, there was no way I would be able to recall it all. All I knew was that there were punches and kicks and knives and guns. My shoulder took a hit. My knives were bloody. The blood dripped down my arms and off my fingertips.

The space was smothered with it, and my breathing was hard, my muscles ached. But when I finally came to and looked around, the narrow opening where several hallways met was literally filled with bodies. Rafe was reloading his gun, as was Dylan. Neither one of them seemed fazed at all by anything I'd done or what had happened there. Rafe just pulled a rag out of his back pocket, tossed it to me, and said, "Wipe your face. There's more."

And together, in a triangle formation, we all turned

down the hallway toward the other gunshots. We only made it about fifty feet in before a door to the right opened, and out stepped the one man I'd hoped I'd never see again in my life. The person that started this all.

Father.

"Matthias. I must say, despite the fact that I have had several casualties at your hand, I love seeing what the years of training have done for you. I have to admit, you're psychologically resistant. I'd always known you were special though. From the day your whore mother brought you here, I knew what you could be. I saw it in you. All those little chats we used to have while you were sleeping, just little suggestions. I had a deal with Orion. He wanted you primed, ready. At that time, I didn't know why. He just paid me a hefty price. He said he was sending a woman and her child my way. And I was to take good care of him, make sure that I was ready for what was to come. I mean, for a few million quid, who wouldn't? I must say, I am impressed. I do not like the sentimental streak of yours, though."

Rafe and Dylan held guns trained on the bodyguards, and I just stared at the man who had been my tormentor, who had killed Gemma, who pumped my mother full of poison and then sold her. And then I looked at my friends, neither one of them wavering, ready to drop every single one of them at a moment's notice.

These guys were my real family. This was what family meant. It didn't matter what the Family had done to me. It didn't matter what my own father had done to me. What mattered was my brothers and what we could accomplish together. What mattered was my love, Gemma.

Father was still talking. "I'm so sorry you've come all this way for nothing. You see, Gemma's already been dispatched promptly and—"

Just having Father say Gemma's name flipped my switch. I didn't even blink. I just raised my gun and shot the man between the eyes.

His bodyguards were close enough to feel his breath and I still got to him. Further proof that no one was invincible. The funniest part was that we said nothing. We merely stepped over the bodies and went after Gemma.

We heard one final gunshot, and then there was silence down the hall.

Oh God, please let her be alive. Please let her be alive. Please don't let her be hurt. Please don't let her pay for my mistakes.

When we turned the corner, guns ready, the three of us ready for anything, we found Gemma and Diana and

Ryan still alive. Banged up, bloody, but still alive. There was a man on top of Diana, and she was trying to shove him off of her frame.

All I heard was the growl that roared out of Rafe. Then Rafe had the guy's body in his hands, throwing him away like he was nothing more than a sack of potatoes. Diana choked and coughed, but she was fine. Rafe pulled her up and dragged her into his arms. Dylan handed Ryan my ammo pack, and I nodded my thanks, but my gaze was only on Gemma.

She was leaning against the wall, eyes closed, chest rising and falling rapidly with every breath she took. "Gemma."

She blinked her eyes open and then frowned. "Matthias? Is that you?"

I nodded. "Yeah. It's me, love. You're okay. Everything's okay."

She still held her guns in her hands, but her hands were trembling. "All this death because I got it wrong. I was wrong. I was so wrong…" Her voice broke on sobs, and I gently disengaged the guns from her hands, tucking them into the back of my cargoes before pulling her to me. "It's okay. There, there. I got you now. I've got you. We've got each other. Nothing's going to hurt you now. It's okay. You're safe now. We're both safe. We've made it out."

As she sobbed, she said, "But Father... He'll just do this again."

I had never been happier in my life to tell her something. "Father's dead. He's never coming after us or anyone else again. I killed him. He's gone for good."

And then Gemma collapsed in my arms. I calmly picked her up. She was mine to take care of now. Forever. Finally, the nightmare was behind us.

18

Gemma

I WOKE up early the next morning but was so warm and comfortable I didn't even move. It was so peaceful to lie in bed. There were no city sounds that reached that high in the penthouse, so it was as quiet as a tomb. No worries about being shot at and no fears that Matthias might not make it back to me. It should've been the most peaceful time of my life.

But all I could think of was that Sabine was dead.

She was a traitor.

The thought should've comforted me. Because of her, members of our team had put their lives in danger.

Matthias could've died. But love didn't work that way. It wasn't something you could just turn on and off. For so many years, Sabine had been the family that I'd lost. Just like Matthias. And I had grieved for her. The guilt of leaving her behind had never left me. It had become a personal mission to right the wrongs of the past. It gave my life purpose.

I didn't know what to do now since that purpose was gone.

"It wasn't your fault." Matthias's voice interrupted my thoughts. "I can see it on your face. You're thinking about her."

"I'm always going to think about her. I'll always wonder if I could have saved her if I'd gotten back sooner. They messed with her mind. Told her lies. If I'd been there—"

"Then it might have happened to you too," Matthias interjected. "You don't have to feel guilty for escaping."

I rolled over into his arms. Warmth surrounded me, and I reveled in it. He somehow always knew exactly what I needed. Whether it was affection or a kick in the ass. Because he was right. I was feeling guilty for that long-ago day. We'd run and left her behind. Nothing could ever change that. And our futures had been decided from that moment on.

"If only we'd been able to take her with us that day."

Matthias squeezed me tighter. "I don't think that would've helped. Father would have found a way to punish us all. Things might've turned out worse for all we know."

Saying the name out loud reminded me. "I can't believe he's dead." It had been the thing we'd always hoped for but never thought we'd actually see. It was like letting go of the boogeyman that had stalked you since childhood.

"Believe it. He is gone, and he'll never hurt us again." Matthias looked down into my eyes. "Nothing will ever hurt you again. I won't allow it."

I leaned up and our lips had just met when there was a loud crash. Matthias jumped up out of the bed, his gun in his hand. I didn't even know where he got it, but I didn't have time to think about it.

"Stay here," he yelled over his shoulder as he ran out of the room.

Like hell I was doing that. He wanted to protect me, a feeling that I understood well. But he was going to have to accept that I was capable of taking care of myself. And that because I loved him, I was going to take care of him, too.

Before I followed him into the hallway, I pulled open the drawer of his desk and took out the gun I'd hid there just yesterday. Matthias wasn't the only one who had heat. He'd closed the door behind him, so I pulled it open and slowly crept into the hall. Oskar was already there, and he motioned for me to stay behind him. I rolled my eyes.

I was surrounded by men who thought I was a delicate flower.

There was another loud crash, so I pushed past Oskar and entered the living room, my eyes scanning for threats. Matthias was on the floor next to the coffee table. His eyes widened when he saw me.

"Gemma, look out!"

I caught a blur of motion in my peripheral vision just as Oskar burst into the room and shoved me out of the way. A figure clad all in black did a spinning roundhouse kick that clocked him right on the side of the face.

"Holy shit!" Oskar stumbled back but recovered pretty quickly for a man of his size.

I knew that kick could take down a Goliath. After all I'd felt it often enough when I was training.

"Everybody stop moving!" I bellowed.

Oskar gaped at me in astonishment as I approached the black clad figure. He stumbled forward as if to grab me, which earned him another kick to the chest.

"Would you stop? They're my friends."

At my scream, the figure in black whirled toward me. A beat later, she snatched the black mask off her face.

"Your friends? *Your friends* held you hostage and put you in the middle of a shoot-out?"

Matthias had staggered to his feet, and he approached, his gun still trained on the intruder.

I sighed, knowing that this explanation was going to take quite a while. "It's complicated."

She smiled. "Isn't it always? Christy was worried. She hadn't heard from you in weeks. I knew you were on a mission, but I figured it wouldn't hurt to check in on things. It looks like it's a good thing I checked up on you. You've always managed to find ways to land in trouble."

I winced at the reminder that I had neglected to call my other mom since before this mission started. Many ORUS agents went months or even years without contact with family. But Andromeda always told me that there were ways around rules if you were creative enough. I'd always left messages for Christy so she'd know that I was okay each month. I hated the thought of her worrying about me.

"Whatever the case, it's good to see you, baby girl."

I opened my arms for a hug. "It's good to see you too, Mom."

Oskar's head had been bouncing between us like he was watching a tennis match. But when he heard that, his mouth fell open. "Mom?" Then he turned to

Andromeda with a look of respect. "Damn, that's one hot mama."

"Okay, ew. Stop that." I punched him until he dropped the pervy look he was aiming at my mother.

Matthias sheathed his gun. "I should have known who you were as soon as you handed me my ass. Your file is impressive, Agent Andromeda."

She winked at him. "You bet your ass it is. Now will someone please tell me what the hell is going on?" Suddenly something crossed her face that looked almost like regret. "And I suppose I should say sorry about the all-American sweetheart that I drop-kicked on my way in. He's still in the hallway. I'm sure he'll wake up soon."

Matthias

THE NEXT HOUR was more pleasant that I would have thought it could be. Andromeda was brash but sincere, and although she was brutal in her interrogation of each of us, it was obviously because she was worried about her daughter.

That was something I could understand.

After all, I worried about Gemma all the time too.

By that time, Noah and Rafe had joined us and were engaged in a conversation with Andromeda about some of the older agents that I never met. They all had stories about the good old days, and I couldn't help teasing them about being old-timers.

"Just wait, kid. One day you'll be the one who's reminiscing about the past." Noah chuckled.

Suddenly Andromeda put her hand to her ear. Then she stood up. "I hate to kick ass and run, but you guys have a visitor."

Gemma looked pained. "You don't have to leave just because someone's coming. Stay. We can tell them to come back later."

I could tell that Gemma didn't want her mom to leave. It was going to be a major priority for me to make sure that she had time with her parents. Not having any myself, I understood better than most how important it was to keep those close family bonds. As I looked around at the guys, I amended the thought. I had a family now. I was lucky enough to see them every day.

Andromeda pulled her daughter in for a hug. "Don't you worry. I'll be back. This is one visitor who won't be denied."

Gemma walked her to the elevator, but Andromeda

put her finger to her ear again as if listening. "I think I'll take the stairs." She pulled open the door to the stairwell and then with one final hug she was gone.

"That was weird," Oskar commented.

He'd been strangely quiet ever since getting kicked in the head. If I'd known that was all it would take to shut him up I would've done it years ago. Although I suspect that pure sexual intoxication had addled his brain. I couldn't exactly fault his taste. Andromeda was a hell of a woman. And I was just as head over heels for her daughter.

The elevator dinged and then the doors opened. Ian stepped out, his eyes moving around in that careful, watchful way that all agents had.

Suddenly Andromeda's quick departure made total sense.

"We need to talk," he said when he saw Noah.

Noah nodded. Then he approached, and when he was about two feet from Ian, he pulled back his arm and punched him in the face.

"What the fuck?" Ian's eyes promised retribution as he held his fingers to his lip.

"You didn't think I'd forgotten you sent an active ORUS agent into my house, did you?" Noah asked.

Ian's eyes still spat fire, but he looked slightly less murderous than before. "You get a pass. Once."

The elevator dinged again, and the doors opened to reveal Jonas and JJ pulling several wheeled suitcases.

When JJ caught sight of them standing around, she paused. Then her eyes fell on Ian's bloody mouth. "Ooh, is this a good time to use my new gun?"

As usual the next few minutes were a round of chaos, which was par for the course whenever JJ was around. Lucia had been in the back feeding the baby but came rushing out when she heard JJ's voice. Squealing and talking a mile minute, the two women went into hyperdrive when Gemma asked to see pictures. JJ yanked out her phone and started showing pictures of the honeymoon, including several naked shots that I was pretty sure Jonas had never intended anyone else to see.

"Good to see that marriage hasn't changed her at all," Oskar laughed. "I was worried for a minute there."

Jonas's cheeks were red, but he shrugged it off. Something I was sure he'd become an expert at since hooking up with JJ. You couldn't hang around that woman and have a shy bone in your body. In fact, Gemma was starting to look like a deer in the headlights, so I waited until I caught her eye and then glanced meaningfully down the hallway toward our room.

I could tell she got my meaning when she yawned

loudly a few minutes later and announced that she needed a nap.

JJ pursed her lips. "A nap? Is that what we're calling it these days? Girl, you're one of the family now. Just say you and Matthias want to bone and stop playing around."

Gemma's cheeks went red, but she gave JJ a high five. "Well, can you blame me? I mean, look at him."

While the girls were *awww*'ing and talking about how sweet it was, behind their backs Oskar pantomimed puking. Ryan almost choked laughing next to him. Not that I cared. Gemma walked into my outstretched arms. I put both my middle fingers up behind her back.

Those guys were just jealous.

Eat your hearts out, fellas.

19

—————

Gemma

I COULD STILL HEAR the sound of the other girls giggling and catcalling as Matthias picked me up and carried me from the room. But none of that could compete with the feeling of being in his arms. I buried my face in his shoulder and breathed in deep, taking in his scent.

I still couldn't believe we'd made it. After everything that happened, we were together. The universe may have beaten us down, but it also brought us back together again, and all I could feel was gratitude.

When we reached our room, Matthias kicked the

door shut and put me down gently, allowing my body to slide along his until my feet touched the ground.

"Are you really tired?" he asked in between desperate kisses to my cheek, ears, and neck.

Shivers rolled through me as his tongue grazed the spot on my collarbone, right below where my pulse pounded.

"Not a chance," I huffed before my fingers tangled in his hair. "We're going to bed but we're definitely not sleeping."

Matthias's soft chuckle vibrated in my ear. "Thank God. I wasn't sure if you'd actually gotten my secret signal or not."

"Oh, I got the signal. The very big signal." My fingers walked their way down his taut abdomen before cupping his cock through his jeans.

I wasn't exaggerating either. Based on the size of the bulge in his pants, Matthias was just as desperate to get me alone as I'd been feeling all day.

His loud groan reverberated through the room and I felt a rush of power at being able to strip him of his control. The man didn't even know how much control he had over me, and it was a relief and a thrill to know that I had that same power over him.

My hand hadn't stopped moving, stroking, and

teasing him beneath his jeans. Suddenly he picked me up and carried me to the bed.

"Someone's impatient."

"I've been waiting for this all day," he gritted out between clenched teeth.

Our lips met in a clash of need, sucking and biting at each other like we couldn't get close enough. That's what it always felt like with him, like I could never get enough.

Honestly, I hoped I never did get enough. I never wanted to know what it was like again to walk through this life without Matthias by my side.

"This is too fast. I have to slow down," he muttered.

I put my hands on his face until he looked at me. "It's not too fast. It's not too anything. It's perfect. You're perfect."

"Don't want to hurt you," he insisted.

I could hear the desperation in his voice but even as he said it, his hands were clawing at my clothes, tugging and pulling each piece until I was completely bare. Only then did he calm, his frantic strokes slowing to soft caresses.

Then he was inside me, stretching and filling every empty space, every void. My head fell back on a gasp at the sudden invasion before I was overcome with pure pleasure. This was perfect. Being filled with Matthias, both body and heart.

When I opened my eyes, I was riveted by the look on Matthias's face. His eyes were closed, and he looked like he'd finally calmed.

Maybe after everything we'd been through, he was finally at peace. Finally at home.

With me.

"I love you so much, Gemma. It's too much for me to even comprehend that you're mine now."

His words filled me with a tremulous kind of hope. That everything really was going to be okay. That the future we'd never dared to dream of would actually come true

"Make love to me, Matthias. Make me believe it."

The erotic dare seemed to spur him to action. His lips pulled into that quirky grin I loved before he thrust his hips, reminding me of where he was. It was amazing how just a slight change in angle could make it feel like he was touching places inside he'd never reached before. But every time we were together it was like the first time all over again. New sensations, new places to explore.

I would never tire of discovering the heights my body could reach in his arms.

"You want me to prove it to you?" he growled. The

low, sexy cadence of his voice instantly turned me on all over again. "Need me to tell you just how hot this pussy makes me?"

I panted as his dirty words ignited a new level of need. This would always be my definition of hot, Matthias growling in my ear as he rode me hard.

"Oh my God!" I couldn't control my response and forgot completely that all of our friends could probably hear us. In that moment, nothing else mattered other than the incredible feeling of taking him so deeply.

His hand came up and cradled my head as he pounded into me, and it brought a startlingly erotic component to things. I felt so safe and protected, a heady feeling for someone like me who was used to kicking ass and taking names on my own. There was a part of me that let go in a way I never had before. And I knew I could do it because it was Matthias and I knew that he loved me. It was a powerful feeling and just the thought set off an orgasm unlike anything I'd ever experienced.

I couldn't even speak, just shook violently as my pussy spasmed around him.

"Fucking hell, Gem. You feel so bloody perfect." Matthias squeezed me tighter, losing even more of his control as he followed over the abyss.

I opened my eyes in time to catch the anguished

look on his face as he came, too. Exhausted and wrung out, I forced my eyes to stay open so I wouldn't miss the view. Seeing him come apart was quickly becoming my new favorite sight.

"Jesus, Gemma. I won't be able to walk for a week. Bloody woman."

I dissolved into giggles at how affronted he sounded. His accent thickened when he was emotional, another thing that I loved because I knew that I was one of the few people to bring it out in him.

"It's okay. I don't plan on us walking anytime soon," I finally managed to say before pulling him down into a kiss.

We had plenty of time. Forever, if I had anything to say about it.

———

Matthias

RESTING ON MY BACK, I willed my heart to slow down. But it was still racing even after getting up to go to the bathroom and clean up. Even after climbing back into bed and pulling Gemma back into my arms.

It was just racing. Maybe I had to accept that this was my new normal. My heart would be in a constant state of agitation. Gemma had me on hyperdrive.

That was love for you.

"I think I'm addicted to you," I whispered against her hair, taking in the soft scent that was uniquely hers. It was impossible for me to be this close to her and not touch her. My fingers were just drawn to her skin. That was an addiction, right?

Love was like an illness. One I'd happily succumbed to.

"If you are, then so am I." Gemma grinned up at me, her impish smile doing things to me that I still couldn't explain.

How was it possible that just seeing her face could make me so happy?

"I can't believe we found our way back to each other after all this time. I'm lucky to have found you again." Her arm that was wrapped around my waist tightened. A mini hug.

"I'm lucky Noah got me out. I can now focus on my future and not my past."

Gemma pulled back slightly and looked up at me. "One question: just how did Noah get you out?"

It wasn't something I spent much time ruminating on lately, but it was true. Noah was uncomfortable with any expression of gratitude on my part and I was, quite frankly, uncomfortable with it, too. I didn't want to talk about our feelings and hug it out. I'd always felt that proving my loyalty to him by being a reliable source of information or backup when he needed it was the kind of thanks a guy like Noah could really appreciate.

But now that I had something more to live for, something to call my own, it occurred to me that a proper thank you wouldn't be out of place. Or maybe that was just the post-sex high talking. But I did feel a rush of gratitude for my friend and for everything he'd risked to save me. Maybe it was time I stopped running from everything and faced it all.

"That's a story the whole family should probably hear. The doc says I need to work on being more open and trusting."

Her smile was gentle as she rubbed my chest. "I know they would love to hear anything you want to tell them. And I'll be there with you. No matter what."

It did help to hear her say it. Because it was easy to say that I should tell the whole story, but actually doing it, well, that would be a whole different ballgame.

As if she could sense my inner turmoil, Gemma leaned up and kissed me on the cheek. "I'm not trying to push you into doing anything you're not ready for. If you don't want to talk about that, then we won't. If you want to tell me the story, then I'll take notes and put anyone who crossed you on my hit list."

That made me smile. "So bloodthirsty."

Her evil grin made my cock stir. "You know you love it."

I flipped her over in a sudden move that left her squealing with laughter. It warmed my heart to see how easy and open things were between us. Despite all the evil I'd done and the things she'd seen me do recently, Gemma wasn't afraid of me. She didn't see the monster that my background molded me into. She saw who I really was underneath it all and accepted me completely.

It made it so much easier to do what I needed to do.

"After our nap is over, I think we should call a family meeting. Get everyone together and talk it out once and for all. I'll never be truly free until I put all this shit in my past. I don't want ORUS to have any hold on me ever again. Not even in my own memories."

She nodded and held a hand against my cheek. "This may sound strange, but I'm proud of you, Matthias."

The pleasure I felt at hearing those words was so profound that I couldn't even maintain eye contact. She would never know what it meant to me to hear those words and feel their truth. My mother and grandmother were the only ones in my past who had ever believed in me and loved me. Over the years, I'd operated to please only myself. The approval of others wasn't something I thought I needed. It was something I'd become accustomed to living without.

But just like in every other way, Gemma was the exception.

"Thank you, baby. I didn't even know I needed that."

She curled her legs up around my hips. "You're welcome. But as for this nap business, does that mean that we aren't done sleeping?"

Her playful tone displayed the slight melancholy that had come over us both. There was a time and place for discussing such emotionally heavy things but in that moment, I just wanted to enjoy being with my love.

"No, we're definitely not done sleeping."

Then I made damn sure everybody in the penthouse could hear just how "awake" we were.

20

Matthias

EVERYONE WAS STARING. Telling my new family about my past seemed like a good idea an hour ago. Now? Not so much.

Then Gemma reached over and took my hand. The simple gesture calmed my roiling stomach and brought me back to what was important. I could do this.

I cleared my throat. "I'm sure you're all wondering why I've called this meeting."

Oskar shifted in his seat, and I smiled, knowing he was trying to decide if he wanted to make a smart comment or not. Noah was next to him with Lucia cuddled against his side. JJ and Jonas were in the armchair, for once being quiet and not bickering. Rafe and Diana were sitting on the floor next to the armchair. I'd asked for everyone to be there, so Ryan and Dylan stood behind the couch, looking uncomfortable as hell.

But if I was going to tell this story, I was only going to tell it once. And everyone needed to hear it.

"Before everything went down, I should have come clean with you guys about my history. My past with the Family was always there, and I knew it would find me again someday. But I never meant for it to involve all of you."

Noah shrugged. "You're one of us, kid. If they come for you, they come for all of us."

There was a chorus of agreement, and I swallowed back an uncharacteristic lump in my throat.

"I never doubted that for a second. But I want to tell everyone the whole story now. You deserve that."

Noah paused and then nodded, sending me a knowing look. The story I would tell was partially his, too. It was important to me that I had his support before I put it out there in the world.

"So, I can't remember a time before I lived with the Family. My mother was one of the working girls, so I was born there and grew up in a warehouse where all the girls lived together."

JJ's soft inhalation was the only indication that my words had shocked her. Lucia's eyes were bright, and I had to look away from her gaze. It was hard enough telling this story without seeing their pity.

"For years, I didn't really understand what was going on around me. I went to school, played with the other children, and came home to do my homework. I never knew my father, but my mum loved me so much that it didn't matter."

I paused, caught off guard by the rush of emotion brought on by thinking of my mum. A normal man wouldn't want to admit it, but I actively tried not to think of her. It was easier to keep all those emotions as part of a past I rarely revisited. But sitting here, talking about her, brought it all back. The rose scent of her perfume, the warmth of her hand on my forehead as she'd push my hair back. Her voice in my ear telling me that she loved me. The knowledge that she was gone, and I would never hear that again.

It was too much.

When the pause stretched a bit too long, Gemma squeezed my hand. "And then I showed up."

Grateful for it, I squeezed her hand back. "And then you showed up. A tiny little girl with huge, scared eyes and the brightest red hair I'd ever seen."

Gemma groaned playfully. "I used to hate it.

Everyone would call me ginger and tug on my braids. Except for you. You took care of me. Kept me safe."

She was making me out to be some kind of hero. But really, she was the one who saved me. Because if I hadn't learned to care for someone else, the Family might have succeeded in turning me into the monster they wanted me to be.

"Not safe enough. After I overheard one of the guards talking about their plans for Gemma, I knew I had to get her out. I had a plan for us to run up north to my grandmother's house. It seems so stupid now, that I actually thought we would get away."

Lucia spoke up then, her voice wobbly. "You were just a little boy, Matthias. You did the best you could."

"She's right," Gemma insisted. "We were so young. I was only eleven, so you must have been... what?"

"Thirteen. Anyway, after we were caught and I saw them throw Gemma in the river, I gave up hope. She was dead, and it was my fault. By the time I was sold to ORUS, I didn't care if I lived or died. But I lived. And then I met Noah."

Noah looked up then, his eyes suspiciously bright. "He was this scrawny kid with a brain like a computer. I'd never met anyone so smart in my life. I started to request him on any missions possible. Then one day, when I really needed him, he was unavailable."

I pick up the story again. "When I knocked on his door that night, I must have looked like hell."

"You did," Noah confirmed gravely.

"All I knew that was that I had woken up shaking and sick, with a wound in my side that had been surgically stitched."

"He had no memory of what had happened to him. All he could remember was the name of the hospital. It was obvious that he'd had some sort of surgery, but we couldn't figure out for what. He'd always been healthy as a horse."

"Luckily, one of the nurses in the hospital owed Noah a favor and was able to get her hands on my chart. The details had been changed, such as name, address, and race but it was the only chart that matched up with the time I was there."

"And that was when I started digging. Someone went through a lot of trouble to make it seem like Matthias was never there." Noah looked grave and his eyes bored into mine.

I knew what he was asking. Did I really want to reveal it all?

"A liver transplant took place the same day on a man in his fifties. AB negative blood type. Same as mine."

"An extremely rare blood type," Noah interjected.

"Based on the chart, it was obvious that I was the

donor. What wasn't clear was why I was taken or how it had happened without me having any knowledge of it."

"Until I realized that someone else I knew had surgery around the same time," Noah continued. "Orion."

Rafe's head snapped up. "What? Did you just say…"

"I did. The old man had no idea how many spies I had at that point. Plenty of other agents he'd fucked over were happy to feed me intel on his whereabouts. About two days after Matthias ended up on my doorstep, I got a tip that Orion was laid up after some type of emergency surgery. That's when I put it all together."

Lucia looked between us, a frown crinkling her forehead. "Put it together? You mean why Matthias was kidnapped?"

"Yes, exactly. Why he was kidnapped and why he had the exact same rare blood type as Orion. Hell, it answered why Matthias was sold to ORUS in the first place. It made sense that the old man wanted to keep his only son close."

Oskar whistled. "Holy shit."

I laughed softly. "That's how I felt when Noah told me what he suspected. At first I wasn't sure what to believe, and I honestly didn't care if he was my old man. I just wanted to find a way to get us out from under his control. So I hacked the ORUS server for the first time.

Found the roster of all active and former agents, info that only Orion had access to. Then I found a video from Orion's private server of his first kill, a senator's son."

Rafe chuckled. "I would have paid money to see that old bastard's face when he realized what you'd done."

"I wasn't there," I admitted.

"He was still recovering from the unexpected surgery. There was no way I was letting Orion anywhere near the kid, so I took the information and went to see him alone. By the time I left, he understood exactly what was at stake if he didn't let Matthias and I both walk free."

"With those files, we could have brought down the whole organization." I still got a chill of satisfaction thinking about it. "If I'd released the roster of all active agents, it would have rendered ORUS effectively useless. Every single open mission would have to be aborted. As much as Orion hated to lose, he couldn't risk that. Not to mention risking his own neck if the world at large saw the video of him murdering the son of a well-beloved senator."

All at once, I was exhausted. Telling the story had been cathartic but draining.

"Blake Security was born on that day. I wasn't sure about anything other than that Noah saved my life and I owed him for it. I've tried to be the best asset I could be."

"Bullshit," Noah roared.

I cringed a little at that. Then he stood, releasing Lucia to come stand next to me. At his motion, I rose awkwardly, still clinging to Gemma's hand.

"You don't owe me shit, and you're not a fucking asset. You're like a brother to me. Get over here."

Before I could process his words, I was enveloped in a hug complete with a pound on the back hard enough to stop my heart. The old Matthias would have frozen in the face of such open emotion, but for once, I allowed myself to feel it.

And to embrace him back.

———

Gemma

AFTER NOAH'S uncharacteristically open show of affection, every one of the guys made a point to come over and embrace Matthias.

He was uncomfortable. I could see it clearly in his

body language and the slightly panicked look in his eyes, but he accepted the love and support patiently.

But I knew all too well that his patience had limits and that it would be best to get him out of there before he hit his quota of human interaction for the day.

"Okay, I think we're going to take a little break after such a heavy conversation. We'll be in our room if anyone needs us."

Lucia opened her arms and pulled me close enough to whisper in my ear. "Thank you for being so good for him. He needs you."

Her approval meant a lot. It was clear this woman was the glue holding this ragtag family together. Matthias loved her like a sister and her opinion meant a lot to him.

Matthias took my arm and allowed me to lead him down the hall to our room. As soon as the door closed, he sat on the bed and let out a heavy sigh.

"That was harder than I thought it would be. But also easier in some ways. I'm glad they know now. My father was a bad man who ruined a lot of lives. For so many years, I was alone with that secret."

I sat on the bed next to him and pulled him into my arms. He came willingly, allowing me to cradle him and stroke his hair. That moment, that quiet moment, was worth every single ounce of suffering I'd gone through to get there. All those years of feeling alone and wondering what my future held, all of it led me to Matthias. To our new family.

To peace.

"You're okay now. And you'll never be alone again." My eyes landed on the Tigger toy sitting on the shelf behind the bed. I tapped him on the shoulder until he sat up.

"Hold on. I want to show you something."

The toy was heavy in my hand. After all these years, it still felt the same. Comforting. Sturdy. My fingers felt along the back for the seam I knew was there. It took a bit of maneuvering, but I got my fingernail underneath the stitch and gently tugged until I could pull the back panel open. When my finger hit metal, I paused. Then I held up the treasure I knew would be inside.

Matthias was watching me curiously. But when he saw what I was holding, his face paled slightly. "Is that—"

"Your grandmother's locket? Yes, it is."

His hands came up to cover his mouth, and he blinked. Then blinked again. "It's been so long since I've seen it. I thought it was lost forever."

Hearing his voice tremble slightly moved me almost to tears. "I thought you were lost forever, too but here we are. That day that we ran, you gave this to me and asked me to keep it safe. I think you were just trying to keep me calm. You'd told me about your grandmother so many times, and you knew it would comfort me."

He reached out and touched the metal, sending the locket spinning on its chain, light bouncing off it in every direction. "After we moved to London the visits to Gran slowed down and then stopped completely. She gave me this the last time I saw her. I wish I'd known then that it would be the last time. But I don't think anyone could have predicted the path my life would take."

"She loved you. I'm sure she was hoping this would tie you to her in some way. Even if she couldn't keep you with her."

He sighed. "I wonder sometimes, how different my life would be if she'd been able to convince my mom to leave me in the countryside with her. I'd have grown up there, maybe herded some sheep. A simple life."

"We can have that now. Let's go to the country and buy some sheep." As expected, that got a laugh from him.

"I think that ship has sailed. I wish I could find her though. The last time I saw her, I was so young. We were already members of the Family by then, so my mother had very limited opportunities to visit her. Over the years, as the organization tightened its control on all of us, there was no more leaving. No more outside world. I only knew her as Gran. I don't know her name or even exactly what part of the country she was from. My memories from that age have faded so much. She told me that the locket would always lead me back home."

Because I could hear the anguish in his voice, I held up the locket again. "It worked, you know. It brought us back to each other. *Home.*"

As I held him in my arms, I sent up one last wish that it would be enough.

21

Gemma

A few weeks later ...

A HORN HONKED as I stepped off the curb and narrowly missed being hit by a lorry. It was so strange being back here, surrounded by the sights and sounds of my childhood. Foreign and familiar all at once.

But I had unfinished business here. And so did Matthias.

"Are you sure you want to do this?" Matthias didn't sound any surer than I felt.

But I wanted to visit Sabine's grave while we were in London.

"It wouldn't feel right to come all this way and not see her, you know?"

By his blank expression, I doubted he understood, but it wouldn't stop him from standing by my side and supporting me. The past few weeks had been chaotic as I adjusted to life on the outside. Now that things at ORUS had changed, for the first time I believed retirement was possible. Noah and Matthias had proven that it could be done. There was life after being in the shadows.

But knowing it was possible and adjusting to living life on my own terms were two different things. It was hard to accept that I was calling all the shots now. With no mission and no protocol, I was on shaky ground each day. With Matthias's help, I was learning how to establish my own goals and missions.

"You don't have to come with me, you know?" I said after we'd been riding along in a taxi silently for a few minutes. I wanted to give him an out. This trip had been hard enough on him.

He didn't look at me, but he squeezed my hand. "I'm coming with you."

And that was that.

The taxi dropped us at the entrance to the cemetery, and before I could do it, Matthias handed over the money. Then we were on the sidewalk, looking up at the entrance gates.

I'd done the research ahead of time and knew where Sabine was buried, so I started walking that way. It was a decent day for it, chilly as London often was, but crisp and clear. The names on the headstones we passed didn't register until I saw the angel carved into the headstone.

Sabine Anne Whitley.

Now that I was here, I had no idea what to do. So I knelt and placed the single flower I'd brought along on the ground before her headstone. Sabine had been buried next to a brother I hadn't even known she had. There were several other headstones around them; I assumed they were other family members. The names were unfamiliar, driving home just how much I hadn't known about my friend.

"I'm so sorry, Sabine."

Matthias dipped his head and stepped away slightly, giving me privacy. I sighed. There were so many things I wanted to say but it seemed so futile. None of it would bring her back. It was true what people said about death, it really made you think about what was important. In this case, rehashing all the ways we'd failed each other no longer mattered. The friend I'd grown up with would have wanted me to be happy in the end. And I wanted the same for her.

"Rest in peace, my friend. I'll never forget you."

I walked a few feet away to where Matthias stood staring out into the distance. His lips curved up at the edges when my arms wrapped around his waist, but I could see the worry in his eyes.

"Are you okay? Did you get to say what you needed to say?"

"I did. I loved her, and I hope she's at peace. Maybe that's stupid after what she did—"

His face relaxed slightly. "It's not stupid. No matter what happened at the end, she was still our Sabine in there somewhere."

It meant more to me than I could say that he got it. Despite her final days, my heart was mourning the person she used to be. The person who was good before the Family corrupted her. That's the person I wanted to remember.

Matthias grabbed my hand. "Let's go back to the hotel. We have a bit of a ride tomorrow. We need to get some rest."

I nodded. We were going to explore the northern English countryside the next day, and Matthias had been really excited about it. This was his chance to revisit some of the places he knew as a young child, before he came to the Family, so it was particularly meaningful. And I was excited because I wanted to share everything with him.

I glanced over at him. There was something different about him. A peace that had never been there before. Whatever it was, it looked good on him.

We left the cemetery hand-in-hand, walking away from our past and toward our future.

———

Matthias

It looked exactly the same.

My head was swimming as the train sped through the verdant hills and valleys of my childhood. Outwardly, I appeared as calm and stoic as usual, but inside I was a mess of emotion.

This trip to England was supposed to be about closure, for both Gemma and me, but in some ways it was opening wounds I hadn't realized I had. The memories I'd long thought buried and forgotten were bursting forth like floodwaters being released. I was desperately trying to paddle along, but eventually I'd given up and was just riding the wave, content to land wherever the storm took me.

Thankfully, Gemma was with me. I could see her profile in the reflection of the train window, head bent reading something on her phone, her brow creased in that adorable frown she always wore while concentrating hard on something.

With anyone else this entire trip would have been torture. Having the scabs ripped off my emotional wounds had left me vulnerable in unexpected ways. Yesterday we'd explored London, and now we were taking the train to Northumberland. Working on old memories of my time with my grandmother, I'd been able to narrow down the likeliest counties where she'd lived. I hadn't slept in weeks, hacking into various companies trying to run down data on elderly residents in each of the identified regions, until I'd gotten one name that fit. Once Gemma had shown me the locket, I'd avoided looking at it for a while. It made me feel things, things I wasn't ready for. But one day, I'd finally pulled it out and examined it.

I wasn't sure exactly what I was looking for; maybe I just wanted to look at it and remember a simpler time. Then I'd noticed the edge of the small picture inside was slightly bent. Peeling the picture away revealed a small map.

Of the county of Northumberland.

My grandmother had been trying to give me a way back to her all along.

Gemma didn't know about any of this yet. In some ways, my search for my past was even harder for her than it was for me. She loved me. It still gave me a thrill just thinking about it. But love made her want the best for me. To be happy. Cared for. She wanted these things for me even more than I wanted them for myself, so I didn't want to tell her about my search and possibly get her hopes up. We'd both had far too much disappointment in our short lives.

She wasn't even old enough to drink yet and she'd already lived through horrors that some didn't see after living for decades.

The whistle of the train brought me out of my thoughts. Gemma looked over at me and smiled.

"Are you ready to explore? This area is more rural, so I looked up some guides online about good trails for walking. This should be a fun day trip."

Her determination to make this fun for me only made me adore her more. She thought that we were there so I could explore my roots a bit and see the countryside I remembered from my childhood. My memories were so sketchy now and just as much imagination as actual recollections, so she thought we were there to fill in the gaps.

"Ready as I'll ever be." I stood with her and we gathered our things and walked off the train. Everyone else scurried off the platform, eager to get where they were going or rushing into the arms of relatives who had come to pick them up.

"That must be our car!" Gemma pointed excitedly to the small black car that was all I could arrange for at such short notice.

"I'll drive," she said quickly.

Despite the fact that it was inconvenient, her fear of letting me drive again was amusing. "Driving on the wrong side of the street is very common when you've been out of the country for as long as I have. I've got it now. Besides you don't even know where we're going."

Ignoring me, Gemma wrenched open the driver's side door. "That's true. But it's going to take me a while to get over the image of you almost running over an old lady with a cane."

I rolled my eyes. "I was nowhere near that lady. So melodramatic. Look under the seat; the key should be there."

The man I arranged to bring the car promised to drop the car off only half an hour before we were due to arrive and leave the key under the seat. I chuckled a little thinking that if we were in New York, the car would have been stolen and probably stripped if left unattended for more than five minutes.

Gemma looked at the directions I pulled up on my phone before we set off. It was a beautiful drive, and my face was practically glued to the window as we ambled down narrow streets and passed farms and animals grazing. Nothing looked familiar in particular, but it felt right.

Like home. Something in me knew we were close.

"Turn here," I instructed as we approached a narrow opening on the right. The hedges hadn't been trimmed and the branches and foliage scraped the car as we passed. The house up ahead was a delightful hodge-podge of shapes. There was a line of laundry blowing in the wind in the field to the left of the house.

Gemma parked the car a few feet in front of a small barn and turned off the engine. "This is an interesting bed and breakfast."

I reached over and grasped her hand. "This isn't a bed and breakfast."

She stared at me for a long moment and then her eyes moistened. "Oh Matthias. Where are we?"

Before I could answer, there was movement behind the line of laundry. An elderly woman appeared, holding an armful of sheets. She paused to shake out a sheet and then took something from her mouth and clipped the fabric to the line.

The white billowing away from her was like a beacon of hope.

My legs didn't listen to the rest of me that warned to be cautious, to take things slow, not to frighten her. No, my legs propelled me from the car with no explanation to Gemma and carried me across the yard toward the beckoning white flag of linen.

When she saw me, the old woman let out a soft cry of alarm. Then she did a double take.

"It can't be," she said finally.

Overcome, I found that I couldn't speak, so I searched my pocket and pulled out the locket. It dangled in the air between us. Her eyes filled with tears, and then her face softened.

"I always knew you'd find your way home."

And when she opened her arms to me, I knew that she was right.

———

THANK YOU for reading the SIN duet.

Have you read Jonas and JJ's story? Keep reading for an excerpt of the steamy and suspenseful, FORCE.

For years I've existed on the edge of the dark, protecting innocents who can't protect themselves. Until... her. Jessica JJ Jones. The bane of my existence. A bright light in the dark. The crack in my armor. A loud, argumentative beautiful crack in my armor.

But first, there's a more immediate concern. JJ is running

scared. And to protect her I might have to break the vow I made years ago.

———

Excerpt of Force © August 2017 M. Malone and Nana Malone

Jessica Jones closed her eyes, exhausted. Day after draining day of pulling double duty while her bestie and partner in crime was on maternity leave was starting to take its toll. Like hell was she going to start complaining, though. If anyone deserved happiness, it was Lucia. Her best friend had been to hell and back and deserved the time off.

JJ could deal. After all Lucia would do it for her. Besides, JJ wasn't letting a prima donna fashion designer run her into the ground and call uncle. She'd rather burn her Jimmy Choos first. She could handle anything their boss Adriana could dish out.

It felt like she'd only shut her eyes for mere seconds before she frowned in her sleep.

Something was wrong. *Very* wrong.

When she peeled her eyes open again, she was in hell.

"Oh my god," she screamed.

But that scream was her first mistake. It meant emptying out her lungs, which meant she needed to breathe... and that meant lungs full of smoke.

It was so hot her hair plastered against her head and her sheets clung to her naked breasts from sweat. Yeah, she slept topless, so what? It had been so hot lately.

Frantic, she looked around the room trying to find the source of heat. It was so dark she couldn't see anything. But she could feel the smoke all around her, cloying and thick, wrapping around her and constricting her lungs.

"Don't panic." The sound of her own voice out loud scared her out of her frozen state. *Fear immobilizes. Anger motivates.* That's right, get pissed off!

If there was anything JJ was good at, it was being hot tempered. What the fuck was smoke doing in her room anyway? She'd just had a goddamned blowout. She needed to charge that color and cut to whatever or whoever was the source of this fire.

Move your ass girly.

She had to move because she was *not* dying in this room. She did not survive her past to die like this. Fuck that noise. Besides, if she died like this, Lucia would resurrect her ass and kill her all over again. After Lucia had survived being stalked and almost killed, JJ had a new appreciation for the meaning of life.

She swung her legs over the side of the bed, letting out a sigh of relief when her toes met the carpet. Now that her eyes had adjusted to the dark somewhat, she could see the faint hint of an orange glow from down the hall. Which meant the fire hadn't reached her room... yet.

But the bedroom door stood open to the hall, which was probably why she could already smell the smoke.

It was weird that the door was open. She always closed the door before going to sleep. It was one of the things Lucia's husband had drilled into her. Noah owned a security company, and his overprotectiveness toward Lucia had spilled over onto JJ. Now she always had one of the annoying, albeit sexy, guys who worked for him trailing her to and from work, and her apartment had been subjected to a thorough security 'review' by Noah's resident IT wizard. Matthias had deemed her place 'merely acceptable.'

JJ was pretty sure they'd have asked her to move if they hadn't known from experience that she didn't take suggestions well. The last thing she needed was some man trying to tell her what to do. Maybe Lucia was okay with that, but she wasn't interested. JJ knew from experience that she didn't want any man having control over her life. Never again. That alpha-asshole shit didn't work for her, so they could shove their over protectiveness where the sun didn't shine.

With a quick glance at the open door, she realized it was actually lucky she'd left it open, otherwise she might not have woken up until the flames were closer. What the hell had woken her? *You can think through that shit after you're safe.* Yeah, good point. She grabbed up her comforter and wrapped herself in the thick fabric, bringing it up over her head as she stepped into a pair of slippers.

How far to the door? The window might be an option if the fire escape hadn't been welded over some years ago. She looked up and then squinted in the darkness. And then she saw the shadow in the hall. The man-sized shadow.

Fuck me. She opened her mouth to scream then reached into her bedside drawer for the nearest weapon she could find. She'd been aiming for the retractable baton she kept in the top drawer. But instead she'd come up with a gag gift from a bachelorette party a couple of years ago. A giant purple vibrator.

What are you gonna do with that? Fuck him to death? Well that was a thought.

"Who the hell are you? And what the fuck are you doing in my apartment?"

He stepped forward slightly, his body still half-hidden outside the door, and JJ raised her makeshift weapon.

"I'm here for you, Jessica. I'm always here for you."

JJ clutched the blanket closer, and her fingers curled around the vibrator as his voice washed over her. The low tone of his words sliced through her veins. That voice. It had been so long since she'd heard that voice. She'd hoped to never hear it again, except in her nightmares.

"How did you find me?"

His chuckle was almost as terrifying as the words that followed. "I never lost you."

JJ screamed and backed up so fast that she stumbled and fell on the bed. The comforter tangled around her and she fought against it, certain the next touch she'd feel would be the last.

Strong hands wrapped around her flailing arms.

"Damn it, you crazy woman, I'm trying to help you!"

It took a few seconds before she recognized the voice, her terror distorting it into the one she feared most. When she finally spoke, her voice was tiny.

"Jonas? Is that you?"

The comforter was pulled back away from her eyes,

and Jonas's handsome face appeared. Jonas Castillo worked for Noah's security company and was a regular fixture in her life. He was routinely assigned to protect Lucia, and by default JJ, during the workweek. She took great pleasure in giving him hell, and he was usually cursing her name or bickering with her.

"Yes, of course it's me."

Before she could question what he was doing there, she felt herself being lifted. She clutched his shoulders automatically, disoriented after her fall. Now she wasn't sure if that had actually happened. Had she been dreaming? It was so hard to tell.

"Jonas, did you see anyone else in the apartment?"

"Like who? Don't you live alone?"

Was that jealousy in his voice? Even under these circumstances, JJ couldn't resist the urge to screw with him a little.

"Actually I don't. We can't leave without my favorite guy."

"Who? And if you have a boyfriend, where is he? Some help he is during an emergency."

"Well, Fluffy has never been much help during emergencies, but he blows the best wet kisses."

Jonas didn't pause. "I'll come back for your dog, I promise. But I have to get you to safety."

It must have been the smoke affecting her brain,

because at first JJ didn't realize what he'd said. It wasn't until they were at the front door that she understood he meant to leave.

"No! I have to get Fluffy!" JJ swatted at his massive chest. She must have surprised him because his arms loosened around her legs, giving her the room she needed to jump down.

"Damn it, JJ! This is serious. We don't have time to stop."

"It'll just take a second." JJ raced back to the guest bedroom and grabbed Fluffy, covering him with the comforter as she ran.

Jonas picked her up as soon as she hit the hallway and ran for the front door. They passed a crew of fire-fighters in the corridor outside her apartment. The smoke was thicker out here, so JJ buried her face in Jonas's shoulder, making sure to keep Fluffy covered too.

When they got outside, Jonas set them down care-fully on the grass, safely away from the building. An EMT approached, and Jonas pointed at JJ. She was going to protest, but dissolved into a coughing fit as soon as she opened her mouth. The young man frowned and knelt on the grass next to her. Then his eyes widened when her comforter slipped and she almost flashed an entire boob at him.

"Hey, eyes up, kid." Jonas glared at him before yanking his shirt off. He put it over JJ's head, and she maneuvered carefully to get her arms in without dropping the comforter completely. If she hadn't felt so crappy, she'd have told him exactly where he could shove it. She didn't need anyone speaking for her.

Just to annoy him, she gave the EMT a bright smile that had the young man blushing furiously. Jonas scowled at both of them.

After a flurry of activity, blood pressure cuffs, and oxygen, they finally left her alone. That's when Jonas got a good look at her again. Her *and* Fluffy.

"A fish? You risked your life to save a fucking fish?"

JJ scooped up Fluffy's bowl protectively. "Fluffy is not just a fish. He's a Japanese fighting fish. A total badass."

Jonas looked like he wanted to strangle her. Normally that was exactly the effect she was going for, but strangely, it wasn't as satisfying as usual.

"Thank you, Jonas. For coming in after me."

He looked as shocked as she felt by her sudden gratitude.

"Of course. It's nothing. The fire department would have gotten to you soon. I just happened to get there first when Matthias said your alarms were triggered."

The talk of alarms brought back memories of the man she'd seen in the smoke. It had happened so fast, and she couldn't be sure what was real and what had been a dream.

"Did you see anyone in there?" At his confused look, JJ clarified, "In my apartment?"

Jonas knelt and looked her in the eye. "Was there someone in there with you, Jessica?"

It was all such a blur, and she didn't like the way he was looking at her. Noah's entire crew was extremely overprotective, so if she said the wrong thing, she'd end up on house arrest with Jonas as her jailor. Plus, it was likely it had all been a dream. Jonas had been in her apartment. He would have seen if anyone else was there. The man in the smoke was nothing more than a shadow from a past she'd rather forget.

"No, I meant in the building. I just want to make sure all my neighbors got out okay."

Jonas looked like he wanted to say something else, but Noah arrived just then with Lucia right behind him.

JJ accepted a hug from her friend, and that was when it really hit her.

"I guess I'm homeless now."

Noah's voice carried from behind Lucia. "You'll stay with us, of course."

JJ's eyes met Jonas's, and she knew he was thinking about her earlier question.

"It's for the best," Jonas said.

She glanced over at Lucia. "Free rent and a house full of hot men. Count me in."

Read FORCE now at malonesquared.com/force

ABOUT THE AUTHORS

NYT & USA Today Bestselling author **M. MALONE** lives in the Washington, D.C. metro area with her three favorite guys, her husband and their two sons. She holds a Master's degree in Business from a prestigious college that would no doubt be scandalized at how she's using her expensive education.

Independently published, her work has appeared on the New York Times and USA Today bestseller lists more than a dozen times. She's now a full-time writer and spends 99.8% of her time in her pajamas. **minxmalone.com**

USA Today Bestselling Author, **NANA MALONE**'s love of all things romance and adventure started with a tattered romantic suspense she borrowed from her cousin on a sultry summer afternoon in Ghana at a precocious thirteen. She's been in love with kick butt heroines ever since.

With her overactive imagination, and channeling her inner Buffy, it was only a matter a time before she started creating her own characters. Waiting for her chance at a job as a ninja assassin, Nana, meantime works out her drama, passion and sass with fictional characters every bit as sassy and kick butt as she thinks she is. **nanamaloneromance.net**